Books by Ron Goulart

THE DAY AFTER THINGS FELL APART
BROKE DOWN ENGINE
THE SWORD SWALLOWER
THE FIRE EATER
GADGET MAN

WHAT'S BECOME OF SCREWLOOSE?

and other inquiries

by RON GOULART

CHARLES SCRIBNER'S SONS ❖ NEW YORK

813.54
G694w

CONTENTS ✹

What's Become of
Screwloose? ☼

I was hardly there when the electric dishwasher grabbed me. It shot its top lid up and tried to submerge my head in hot soapy water. Twisting, I kneed its smooth desert-colored front surface and managed to yank its cord free of the kitchen wall plug. The machine kept working, pumping burning water up at me, clutching at my shoulders with some kind of wiry tentacles. I grunted, snapped both its arms off me for a second. I spun the heavy machine away from me. I dodged it, hopping across the bright parquet of the afternoon kitchen.

The dishwasher came rolling after me, arms out-stretched. I grabbed up a blowmold kitchen stool and thrust it at the machine's running wheels. The dish-washer tripped, fell over on its side and splashed scalding sudsy water all around. I ran for the sundeck, my right hand reaching up under my jacket toward my holster.

Upright again, the dishwasher was rolling my way on its little wheels. Behind me was the Pacific Ocean, about three hundred feet straight down. I drew out my laser pistol and waited, aiming.

Soapy water had splashed out here on the bright black topping of the wide deck, and as the dishwasher came humming from the kitchen into the sunlight, it took a skid. Its arms clutched air, flapped, and it whirled by me, wild. It hit the redwood rail and went right on through, falling toward the ocean, followed by splintered wood. The machine's grasping arms caused it to somersault once in the air before it slammed into the water. After the giant splash came big bubbles.

Three white gulls came skimming in low over the water. They danced a second or two over the last of the bubbles and then glided up into the clear air. I hung up my laser gun and went, carefully, back into the beach cottage.

The stove looked like it could be nasty in a fight, but apparently it wasn't gimmicked. Nothing else in Mary Redland's empty beach house came for me.

In the beam ceiling living room the phone on the missing girl's marble top coffee table began to buzz. I watched it, approaching it from the side. It looked to be only a phone and I decided to switch it on and answer.

"Tom," said the lank dark young man who appeared on the saucer-size view screen, "is she there?"

"No, Oliver," I told him. "At least, I don't think so. I just arrived." I glanced toward the view window, which showed the quiet ocean.

"Tom, you look distracted," said Oliver Bentancourt, our client.

Out in the ocean I noticed the dishwasher swimming out to sea. Doing a fair Australian crawl with those unexpected arms. "I was looking at the dishwasher."

"How's that going to help us find out where Mary's been for the last two days?"

I sat on the paisley patterned white nauga sofa and said, "This dishwasher is out in the Pacific, swimming."

"Oh, you mean some guy who works in a restaurant. Who is he?"

"No, I mean an appliance, square squatty thing about half my size," I said. I took another look at the bright ocean. The machine was quite far out now and had switched to a rapid back stroke.

"How can it swim?"

"It has little arms," I said.

Bentancourt rubbed a lean hand over his eyes. "I guess you're not kidding, Tom. I don't know. Maybe it's because of her late father that she's got an odd machine there. I don't know. Mary is, well, she isn't like anyone I've known before. I really didn't want to consult your boss, you know. But since you and I have been friends since catechism class days I figured you wouldn't be working for Stanley Pope unless he was okay. Where is Mary?"

"Easy now. We'll find her. Stanley Pope specializes in cases that are a little eccentric."

"I don't want to use the police," said Bentancourt. "You know, because Mary has a pretty unhappy medical record. Well, psychological record rather. She's still in therapy. The police aren't too understanding."

"Right."

"I've called her friends, such as they are. I even tried to see if anybody was still at the old family place." He hid his eyes again for a moment. "She's not there? I mean, she didn't take something again?"

"No," I said, though I wasn't certain yet.

"Okay," said Bentancourt. "I'm only on my coffee break here at the office. I'll call you later on tonight." He nodded, smiled a quick smile and faded off the screen.

The dishwasher was only a speck now, a desert-colored dot on the straight edge of the ocean. I rubbed my chin, then scratched my chest with both hands. I went all through the three-room beach house I'd let myself into and Mary Redland was not there. Nothing I found told me where she might be.

Pope was out on his court playing tennis with a robot. I sat down on one of the wrought-iron benches ringing the green clay. Down through the trees and housetops I could see a flock of sailboats on Sausalito's piece of the Bay.

"I'm perfecting my serve," Pope called to me. He flung a fuzzy white ball straight up, kept his eye on it, whapped it over the net.

"You're using a badminton racket," I pointed out.

The robot was shaped like a water heater and had four arms. It rolled after the served tennis ball and sucked it up off the court with a little nozzle.

Pope blinked. Wrinkles ran up his high forehead and got lost in his tight curly black hair. "Huh?" New rings joined those under his wide, circled eyes.

"Badminton racket." I inclined my head in its direction.

He scrutinized the racket, nodded. "I must have left the tennis racket in the copter."

"Copter?"

"I was test flying a new copter." He waved at the robot. "Game's over."

"I thought you gave up on copters."

"They have a tendency to crash," he said, "into the Golden Gate Bridge."

"When you're piloting."

"Anyway, I decided to give copters one more chance."

"And?"

"This one crashed into the Golden Gate Bridge."

I noticed the robot was speeding toward the tennis net. "Your robot thinks he just lost the game."

"Huh?"

"He's going to jump over the net and congratulate you."

Pope turned. He was a lean, middle-sized man, nearly as dark as I am. "Don't," he yelled as the robot leaped up into the air.

The tennis-playing machine didn't quite clear the net. It tumbled over front first with a clang, scattering tennis balls.

"Gadgets," said Pope. He ran to the fallen robot and helped it up. "I had a chance to inherit a hundred acres of soy beans in the San Joaquin Valley, Tom. Instead I surrounded myself with gadgets."

"Sorry, sorry," said the robot, feeling itself for damages with all its hands.

Pope left the machine and came over on the grass with me. "What about this missing girl? Mary Redman."

"Redland."

"I worry about all these gadgets the way some people worry about pets. I get nervous and concerned when they fall down." He blinked again and new rings appeared around his eyes. "What do I take at six o'clock?"

I reached a bottle of blue spansules out of my jacket pocket. "Two of these."

"Well, I probably would have worried about soy beans, too." Pope shook two spansules into his palm, frowned. "Except soy beans don't fall down as much. Any trace of the girl?"

"No," I said. "But her dishwashing machine tried to kill me."

He swallowed, rubbed his forefinger along the side of his beaked nose. "Huh? Give me all the details."

I described what had happened when I'd gone to look for the girl up beyond Stinson Beach.

Absently Pope undid his white tennis shorts and let them drop. "I should have gone over there with you. Why didn't I?"

"You had to go to San Francisco, remember."

"Oh, yes. One of my former wives is after more alimony. The second one, right?"

"No, the third," I said. "Why are you taking off your clothes?"

"Changing for dinner."

"You're still outside."

"Huh?" Pope bent and retrieved the fallen shorts, folded them under his arm with his badminton racket. "I had a chance to go into the fishmeal business once. There's a lot less pressure in the fishmeal business than in the private investigation field. Right?"

"I haven't seen any statistics." We continued across his slightly overgrown two-acre backyard, moving in the direction of Pope's big transplanted Victorian house. "What did that homicidal dishwasher remind you of?

You did a particular kind of reaction take when I mentioned it."

"Huh?" Pope stroked his nose. "Something I can't quite remember. But it ties in with this Mary Redland business." He stopped walking. "I really like the odd cases, Tom. Most of what we do know is simple electronic stuff. Bugging, counterbugging, siphoning of computer information. Back in the 1970s, when you were still in school someplace, there were more odd things to work on. Her father."

"Mary Redland's father?"

"Right. He was a servomechanism tycoon, wasn't he?"

"That and teaching machines," I said. "My friend Bentancourt says Mary didn't talk much about her father. He died a year or so ago, in an autosonic jet crash. I know the few times I met her she didn't talk about the past at all."

"This name that scared her, upset her?"

"Screwloose," I told him.

"Right. A nickname for somebody maybe. Your friend hasn't any notions?"

"Nothing new since he consulted us this morning, no."

"Mary Redland is in a therapy group over in Frisco, right? How long?"

"Three months. And, according to Bentancourt, she mentioned the name Screwloose during a session at this Dollfuss Center. He's not in the group with her, but she told Bentancourt about it afterwards. Because it scared her. A silly name but she was unsettled. Apparently that was all she was able to remember, just the name or whatever it is. Screwloose. Bentancourt figures maybe she remembered something else day before yesterday. Maybe that's why she took off."

"Why should she be remembering things?" asked Pope as we climbed the wide wooden back stairs of his vast rococo white house. "Did Bentancourt say she'd lost her memory at some point?"

"No, but she's had a breakdown or two and there seem to be certain things she has trouble recalling."

"Slender girl, isn't she?"

"He showed you her picture."

"I know. Willowy, tall. Blonde," said Pope. "Thin women tend to be twitchy. My second wife was."

"Third," I said. "Your second wife was a plump redhead with dimples."

Pope sighed. We were in the kitchen. "Maybe I should have stayed with her and taken up soy beans. Huh. Go to the Dollfuss Center and sit in on that group therapy session. Mary Redland was going every Tuesday and Thursday night at eight, wasn't she?"

"Yes. There's a session tonight. You figure she may show up there, even though she's been out of view for two days?"

"No. I want you to find out what reminded her of Screwloose." He nodded at his refrigerator and it opened and handed him out a cold bottle of ale.

Pope gestured uphill at the houseboat after I'd given him a verbal report on my visit to the group therapy session the night before. "We'll go up to Past after breakfast. Did I order orange juice?"

We were under a metal umbrella out on a plank shelf over the edge of the Bay, at a restaurant called The Ruins of Tiburon Tommy's. "Tomato," I said. I removed a pill from a box I carried in my left trouser pocket and put it on the edge of his soycafe saucer.

"I'm sorry I didn't turn up anything on Screwloose," I said. "Why Past?"

"Something," said Pope. He noticed a plate of plankton griddle cakes in front of him on the table. "I like to use Evelynski to suppliment my memory sometimes."

"Didn't they indict Evelynski for siphoning classified information out of the California State Credit Computer?"

"They couldn't. No evidence."

"I thought they had evidence."

"Evelynski managed to siphon off all that, too." Pope was wearing a buff-colored overall suit today. He rubbed his palms on his knees and the material gave off a purring sound. "Go back on what you told me about last night. At the therapy session you said one of the group talked about Mary. He said something about how her late father paid a lot of attention to her, especially to her education?"

"Yes, a big jovial pink guy in his middle forties. His name is Chuck Mogul," I answered. "When I asked him if he knew her he said he'd only read about her family a lot in the society columns. Years ago. Dr. Dollfuss is an admirer of yours, otherwise they probably wouldn't have let me sit in. He mentioned your eclectic mind."

"Right." Pope looked once more at the pancakes, then stood. "Let's go up and consult Evelynski."

Past is a private research organization. When all the houseboats were cleared out of the waters around Sausalito back in the 1970s, Cosmo Evelynski had one moved to a lot in the low rolling hills of Tiburon. The big red-and-white boat served now as the top floor of his archives, with ten more floors sunk down into the hillside.

Evelynski's office was in the living room of the old houseboat, and we found him there dropping punch cards into an electric wastebasket. The basket would chew up a card, making a lopsided growling sound. Then it would spew the fragments back out at Evelynski.

Evelynski was sitting on a low wicker stool, a confetti of shreds on the hardwood floor around him. "On the fritz," he said. He was a tall man in his low forties, short-haired and mildly rustic-looking.

Pope took a seat on a plaid ottoman. The rings around his eyes were flickering. "About twenty years ago, sometime in the late 70s or early 80s," he said, "something like four men who were all prominent in the servomechanism field died. I've been trying to remember the details."

"Hello, Tom," Evelynski said to me. He kicked the wastebasket off with his left foot. "You're thinking about a murder case, Stanley?"

Pope said, "It's not on record as such. All four of these guys died in a six-month period, all in accidents. They were, though nothing much was made of it as I recall, the chief competitors of what's his name. Donald B. Redland. Mary Redland's father."

"Redland of United/Tech?" Evelynski stood up and crossed to a dumb waiter in the wall.

Pope nodded. "In one of these accidental deaths there was something . . . something about an eyewitness. Little boy, nobody believed. He claimed he'd seen a soft-drink machine push the victim off the edge of a bluff in Muir Woods someplace. A foggy day, nobody else saw anything."

"The dishwasher," I said.

"Reminded me," said Pope.

Evelynski opened the door to the shaft and yelled,

"Freak Accidents, 1978 through 1982. Also Redland, Donald Bascomb. Muir Woods, accidents, vicinity, 1978 through 1982. Servomech industry, obits, same period. Anything else you can think of." He let the small white door flap shut. "I've dug down two more floors since you guys were here last."

"Did you fix that computer who would only take requests given in classical Greek?" asked Pope.

"He just outgrew it. He was new then and showing off. You know, the runt in the pack." Evelynski made his way around the circular room and stood next to the mouth of a metal chute. Far down under us a faint fluttering whir had started. In another thirty seconds file folders, tape reels, punch cards, loose clippings and glossy photos poured out into Evelynski's arms. "Here," he said and dropped the wad of material on Pope's lap.

Three newspaper clippings fell in the process. I reached them off the hook rug and glanced at them. The headline on the largest clipping, a half-page with photo, read: "Peninsula Girl Has a Special Sort of Teacher." The girl, six then, was Mary Redland and her special tutor was an android teacher especially designed by her father, Donald B. Redland, and built under his supervision at United/Tech near Sunnyvale. The story said Mary liked the teaching robot "an awful lot" and the family nickname for him was Professor Screwloose. There was a picture of Mary and the android in a bright playroom. I held the clipping out to Pope. "Here's Screwloose," I said.

"Oh, so?" He took the clipping.

"Also Chuck Mogul," I added.

"You're getting slipshod, Tom," said Pope. "Here one of the six people you spent two hours with last night is an android and you didn't tumble to it."

"Nope," I admitted. "He's got a lot of believability. He struck me as a phoney, but a human phoney."

Pope tapped the photo. "This was taken at the Redland place down on the Peninsula, wasn't it?"

"That's right," I said. "The estate's been empty since Redland was killed, nobody's living there. But supposedly it's still guarded by a lot of Redland-invented mechanisms."

"Huh," said Pope. He rolled up the piece of newspaper and rubbed it across the tip of his sharp nose. "I wonder if Mary Redland's gone there. What she's trying to remember has to do with this damn android and probably with that old house."

"I'd better drive over there and check," I said.

"After we go through the rest of this stuff, yes," said Pope. "Stop at my place and gather up some tools for jobbing the burglar alarms. We have something or other for stunning robots, don't we?"

"Yes. Do you want to come along this time?"

"No, I want to call on Chuck Mogul," said Pope. "You said the Dollfuss records show him with a San Francisco address?"

"Yes, Telegraph Hill." I wrote the address on a memo slip.

"I want to ask him why he's no longer Screwloose," said Pope.

Nothing was working at the Redland estate. I'd parked my landcar three hundred yards beyond the front stone wall, in the shadows of a grove of black oaks. The day was ending early and a gray prickly mist was tumbling down out of the darkening sky as I walked carefully toward the front gates. The gates were twice my height and twisted into patterns of Rs and grape leaves. The gate was the kind that gave off an alarm ring if touched and an electric wire netting grew up to six inches above the high thick stone wall. Floodlights had been aimed at the cleared ground on the visitor's side of the gate and just on the other side of the wrought iron a black police dog crouched, fangs bared.

But none of it was working. The floodlights weren't on, the robot dog was silent and there was no life in his vinyl eyes. The gates had swung a few feet open. I'd been prepared to try to gimmick the alarm system and pick any locks I ran into. I had a brown nearleather attaché case under my arm. It wasn't necessary. I walked through the gates.

The mist fell and rolled, thickening. Far away, back on the highway, a diesel truck groaned by. In passing the mechanical watchdog I brushed against him and he fell over sideways. I could see the shape of the house now, a quarter of a mile away. Cupolas and spires and weathercocks jabbing free of the mist. The main house was three stories, twenty-five rooms. There was supposed to be a six-car garage with chauffeur's suite, a copter hangar and two small guest houses beyond and behind the main house.

The acres of grass had been recently cut. It had a damp fresh-cropped smell. The trees, hundreds of birches and willows and pines, were less cared for. Approaching the Redland house I saw an android sprawled in the brush. He was a gardening robot and he looked to have fallen from a ladder while pruning. He was broken and beginning to rust. His bent hand still clutched a pair of shears, orange now from exposure.

There was only darkness in the main house. I went full around it, listening. I crossed a stable yard in back of the big house and saw light. A fluttering unsteady glow coming from a cottage deep among willows. I went toward that.

A metal plate screwed to the cottage door said: Miss Mary Redland/Her Playhouse. I knocked. The motion of my knocking pushed the door open. Inside the small room was Mary. She was sitting in a low wood chair, her legs bent up and tight together. On a child-size desk beside her was a kerosene lantern with a sooty smoke fluming up from it.

"Hello, Mary," I said.

She looked up, nodded, smiled very faintly and briefly. "Hello, Tom."

"This is where you've been?"

"Most of the time." Her prettiness seemed to come and go on her face, wavering like the lantern light. "I guess Ollie hired you to come looking for me."

"That's right." I took a lopsided sofa chair for a seat. There were shelves climbing the walls, cluttered with toys. Simple stuffed toys and complex mechanical ones. Below the shelves were teaching machines and film viewers, spools of history and math piled atop them.

"Somebody is always and continually looking for me," said the girl. "Since always." She locked her slim hands over one knee. "I remembered some things and came back here to think about them. To reflect, more or less."

I watched her, not saying anything.

"They never," said Mary, "thought I'd remember. And I didn't, actually, quite remember for a long time. Then I began to."

I stayed quiet.

"Fifteen. No, twenty. Twenty years ago almost," said Mary. "When I was about six years old. Then my father and one other man who worked for him. They're both dead now. I suppose that's funny. Twenty years ago they killed four people."

"Rivals," I said. "People your father couldn't buy out?"

"His ambition was to become much bigger. He did, too," said Mary. "They, my father and the other man, came up with a fine and simple idea. Not something that would seem simple to me or possibly to you, but to them. He could have kept trying to deal with them financially, buy them. Except this new idea was simpler and not as expensive. So they figured out how to adapt some of their fine machines and mechanisms. Adapt them to kill people. Not in any obvious ways, though. To push them out of windows or arrange accidents. There's a funny side to that, too, being killed by your refrigerator or your color TV console."

I said, "I met one of those machines."

"Yes, I guess a few of them are still around," she said, "to keep an eye on me. I gave up trying to avoid all the mechanisms Dad thought should keep track of me. You probably saw it in that beach house Dad bought for me three years ago."

"That's right."

Mary said, "The problem was, the problem was I walked in."

"On a killing?"

She shook her head. "No, on the planning of one. They were very thorough. They made charts and diagrams, everything very efficient. Maybe that's how you should kill people, carefully and with a good deal of thought and deliberation. I walked in. It was up there at the big house. In Dad's den, which was supposed to be private. I didn't always pay attention to that kind of restriction then. I was six and they'd not bothered to lock the door this one time. I walked in, very silent and way across the room from them. Dad was at his long wide work table, drafting table, and they were talking about it. I listened for a long while until they noticed me." The mist was thick at the little room's round leaded windows. "At first they, Dad especially, tried to convince me I hadn't heard anything or that it was just a game. The problem was, you see, they went right ahead and killed the man. So I asked about it." She stood and wandered to the low black and gray machines. "This is where they did it."

"They worked to make you forget?"

"Yes," said Mary finally. "It used to be called—what was it?—brainwashing. It wasn't going to hurt, Dad promised. Seems to me, it seems to me it took them weeks to do. They used these machines and some others." She paused and took a sharp inward breath. "And my tutor. I had an android. A nice affable robot who taught me and read stories and was nice. I called him Professor Screwloose. I don't know why, something Dad said once is where I got the name, I think. He helped them do it and after that he was gone, sent someplace else. For years I forgot, didn't remember. Except it started trying to come back. You know, I had some problems. Yes. I went into therapy finally and I really began to remember." She turned to me. "He was there, though I didn't realize it at first."

"Screwloose," I said.

"Yes," she said. "Calling himself Chuck Mogul and passing for human. I guess Dad had programmed him to keep watch on me. Even with Dad gone nobody turned poor Screwloose off. He's still hanging around, watching after me. Protecting me. I suppose he's anxious to keep me from remembering, even though it doesn't make much difference now."

"You paint me as not too nice a guy," said Chuck Mogul. He came into the cottage, grinning. There was a black pistol in his believable right hand. "Gee, Mary. We have meant nothing but good for you."

"It's all over, Professor Screwloose." She leaned against the black machines.

"No, I don't feel that," said the Screwloose android. "Gosh, your dad, God bless him and keep him, set me up swell, Mary. With funds and a nice place on Telegraph Hill in San Francisco. All I have to do, as long as I live, is look after you. Not only to keep you from thinking about some unpleasant things that might have happened when you were a cute little tousle-headed kid. No, I'm devoted to seeing to it you have a calm, pleasant life always."

"Good Christ," said the girl. "My father was enough. I don't want any more sweet concern. I'm me now, full-grown and I don't want you."

"Gosh, Mary," said Screwloose. "Don't talk like that. I'm always going to be around. I'm, gee, I'm made that way, honey."

"You shouldn't have," I said, "gotten so close. Shouldn't have gone to the therapy sessions."

The android agreed. "I debated a lot about that. Gosh, but I was worried. About what she might blurt out there in front of the others. So I took a risk, pulled a few strings and got in the same group with her. No, I have to admit that little plan didn't work so good."

"Seeing you again helped me remember," said Mary.

"Well," said Screwloose, "no long-range harm done. We only have to fix your mind up again, Mary, and you'll forget all this nasty stuff. Your dad taught me how and I can do it myself."

"No," said the girl.

I asked, "Me, too?"

Screwloose replied, "No, you we'll have to kill in some accidental-looking way. I was hoping you'd get drowned at Stinson Beach. I only just tonight figured Mary might have come back here, for sentimental reasons. Had I thought of it earlier I would have beat you to it. Again, gee, there's no real harm done. I know all kinds of easy ways to kill people."

The playhouse door quietly opened again and Pope dived in. He held a cross-shaped tire iron. His first swing knocked Screwloose's pistol away. Pope's next two blows were to the android's head and they caused him to fall over with an outflung jerking. "Gosh," said the android. He began a slow tumble down to the floor. He was making loud whirring sounds and oily smoke came from his nostrils and mouth.

"The reason I was a little late," said Pope. "I bumped into some landcars on the highway. It was a produce truck full of synthetic tangerines, actually. I'd been trailing Screwloose since he left his place in Frisco. I lost him after the collision but figured he'd head here. I picked him up again at the gates. None of the alarms are working, by the way."

"I turned everything off," said Mary, leaving the area of the teaching machines. "I don't like all that stuff much."

"You just happen to be carrying a tire iron?" I asked Pope.

"Actually," he said, rings forming around his wide eyes, "I had a flat tire, too. After one of the truck drivers kicked my car. That's what threw my timing off."

"Your timing was fine," I said.

"This is Mary Redland, huh?" Pope asked, nodding at the girl. "You've been here hiding out?"

"Not hiding out, thinking, trying to remember. I wanted to remember everything. I wanted to remember what they had done to me," said the girl. "But I'm still not sure why they did it."

"Because we loved you," said Screwloose. His head began to come apart.

✵ Junior Partner

Sometimes the street lights come on at six o'clock and sometimes not until nearly eight. Tonight they've come on at 7:35. Eventually I'll have to leave here. I've never really liked my father's office. I don't like it now that it's mine. I can't leave through the outer offices. I can't do that. And the fire escape is attached to the next office over. There's a ledge but it's four stories to the ground and I have a pretty strong fear of heights. That was one of the failings of mine that my father never tired of pointing out.

He's been dead nearly a month now. There aren't any pictures of him here. His vanity didn't run to the pictorial. Still, I can feel him all over this big damn room. The lousy spears and masks and all the other crap he acquired on his vacations. His vacation always came in July and August. Two months away and always back in time to send me off to whatever new school he'd picked.

Once when I was fourteen I came across one of his catalogues of military academies and there was a pinhole next to the name of the school I was going to that year. As though he'd just flipped the book open and stuck a pin with his eyes closed and that was why I was going to school in Arizona. But then I figured he'd done that just to get at me. I realized he wouldn't leave something like the directing of my life up to chance. April Fool pranks were always in season with him.

My father was five feet six inches tall. He always gave his height in inches, though. Sixty-six inches. He'd lost all his hair in his early twenties, during the period when he was bumming around Arabia or someplace and screwing the people out of whatever it was they had to be screwed out of. He and my mother separated when I was only a few months old and he kept me.

My mother died when I was eighteen. I don't remember what she looked like and I've never seen a picture of her. My father never mentioned her. I knew she'd died because there were small stories in all the San Francisco papers here. She died in Connecticut. In Westport. There were four papers here in those days I think. That was before the war. I'm nearly forty now.

There's a birthdate on my records but I've never really been sure it's right. Although my father may have been using some kind of purloined-letter psychology on me and let me have the real facts. I know I've never really believed him or trusted him from the time I was four or five. As far back as then I have always tried to check him up and prove him wrong. In Elko, Nevada, where I was supposed to have been born, they had no record of it at the city hall. My father and mother did live there in the early twenties, that I found out from old city directories.

It was probably a good thing he kept me scattered across the country. If I'd been here in San Francisco I would have spent all my time checking into the things he'd told me. I found that by the time I got to college I was an expert in research.

After I got out of the army after the war I wanted to get a teaching position at some small junior college outside of California. But somehow I ended up here. I started off as promotion manager of Arlen Keever Enterprises. That's my father. Arlen Keever, Sr. I, of course, am junior.

Every morning sharp at 8:45 all our employees showed up. Only once, the time Hollis fell off the cable car and broke his leg, was anyone late. Our employees, roughly 150 of them, split their lunches up. Half of them went from 12 to 12:45, the rest from 1 to 1:45. According to my father, only female employees are entitled to a coffee break, under the law. So every morning at 10:05 half the girls went to coffee. At 10:25 they came back. The rest went to coffee at 10:30 and came back at 10:50. A similar schedule held for the afternoon break.

That's how things ran until my father fell down dead right under the Haitian drums on the wall over there. Since I've assumed the running of Keever Enterprises we've been operating in what my father would have called a slipshod and haphazard manner.

As far as I can tell, and I know how to make an impressive variety of charts and graphs to check this sort of thing, our efficiency and production haven't dropped off since my father's methods stopped being used.

About five weeks ago, when he began to realize he was dying, my father explained his system to me in detail. I'd heard his rules and maxims as far back as I can remember. I'm sure he circled my crib and ran off some of his chats on virtue, punctuality, thrift and the rest. But the system was new to me.

Being a junior partner in Keever Enterprises, I was allowed a full hour for lunch. When I came back that particular day there was a memo on my desk from my father.

"Junior," it said. "As soon as you straggle back from lunch please come and ask Miss Spaulding if you can see me. I have some urgent business I want to chat with you about. If you have been drinking please take one of the mints I've left on your desk, which could stand a good reorganization, by the way."

There were two white afterdinner mints sitting next to my In box. The only other thing on the desk top was a file of letters I'd been going through. I put it in a file drawer and, dusting the desk top with my handkerchief, went out to Miss Spaulding's desk.

My father was free and after Miss Spaulding smiled and tilted her head at his door I went up to it and knocked. My knock was two short, three long.

"Enter, enter," called my father.

I did. "You wanted to see me, sir."

"That's right, junior. You figured my memorandum

out perfectly. You're getting to be almost efficient. How's your wife?"

I've been divorced for over a year. "I don't hear from her. I send the alimony checks to her bank and that's it."

"I'm not in very good shape," he said.

I'd suspected something might be wrong with him. He wasn't circling his desk, just sitting back in his swivel chair, his hands folded in his lap. "What is it?" I asked him.

"I've talked to Dr. Weiner and he says it's my old timepiece."

My father rarely referred directly to any part of the body. "Your heart?"

"What the heck else would I mean?" He pulled a cigar out of the black cigar humidor and screwed the lid back on. "I have a hunch I may be passing along beyond soon, junior."

I felt an odd pain across my chest. "You're not serious?"

"Do I have a reputation for sick humor?" His face wrinkled up. "Yes, I'm serious."

"But you can take it easy. Rest. Go to the desert. People do things like that," I said. "And it adds years to your life."

"Fiddle," he said. "Isn't your real concern over whether or not you can step into my boots and do the job? You don't care if I'm here or over in glory playing in the angel band. Do you?"

"Of course I care, sir." I began to wonder if this was another one of his games.

"Your grandfather was a professional wrestler before he went into the cattle business," he said, slowly pushing himself back from his desk. "I've seen your grandmother bulldog a steer unaided. Does that suggest anything to you?"

"They must have had some great family quarrels."

He gave a strong push and was free of his desk and chair and standing. "Your ancestors were tough, courageous people. Pioneer types. You know that one of our family was a close friend of Robert Burns. And poets weren't pansies in those days."

"I know, sir."

"It's time, junior," said my father, getting his hands locked behind him, "that you start giving a hand to heredity. When I've moved on I want you to run the show here, mind the store while your pop's out on the road.

I had a feeling he might be serious. He never called himself my pop unless he was in a straight mood. I said, "You don't have to talk like this, sir. I'm sure you'll live a long time."

"With a bum ticker? Like heck I will." He was at one of the wall safes. The one behind the African mask on the far wall. "You'll have to memorize the combinations to the safes. It's time for you to know them." He swung the safe open and took out an old book, bound in some kind of soft pale yellow leather. "I picked this up in Europe some thirty years ago." He came slowly back to his desk and dropped the book on it. "Now for the other safe." He stood still for almost three minutes, breathing softly through his mouth. Then he crossed slowly to the big stand-up safe next to the bookcases. "Whatever you do, butterfingers, don't drop the tray. I keep these things activated all the time. It saves work and trouble."

He smiled to himself, opened the safe and took out a cafeteria-sized tray and brought it back to his desk.

There seemed to be a set of chess pieces or, more likely, two sets, on the tray. They weren't chessmen, but toy soldiers of some kind. I'm nearsighted and I had to get my glasses out to take a good look at the little figurines.

By that time my father was standing in front of his desk, looking at the tray. "The staff," he said.

"What are they, sir? From a doll house?"

"Take a good look," he said.

I bent down. The figures were dressed in business suits and dresses and skirts. "Very fine workmanship."

"Thank you. I made them myself. You'll find the directions and the recipes in that book."

"You want me to make dolls?"

"The faces," said my father. "Squint, junior. See the faces."

I guess I'd been avoiding that. "Hey. There's Beckman. And Tom Hockford and Larry O'Brien. And Nancy Ferrier and. . . ." I stopped. There was a four-inch-high doll replica of about half the people who worked for us. I looked up at my father. "You have them for everyone on the floor?"

He nodded. "Our entire staff, yes."

"It's certainly an interesting hobby, sir," I said. "I didn't know you went in for this sort of thing."

"Hobby, my knee," he said, looking at the big wall clock. The clock is just like a schoolroom clock, all our clocks are. The hands jumped to 1:40 and my father went around behind his desk. "Time for them to start coming back." He twisted the humidor lid the wrong way and a small drawer clicked out. There was a packet of orange powder in it. "The set of Conrad on the shelf over there is fake. You'll find more of this stuff," he jiggled the packet, "in there. About a year's supply left.

Recipe's in this book when you run out. I find making up a two-year supply each time is a good idea. It stays effective about that long."

"I see."

Opening a side drawer of his desk he pulled it out completely. He set the drawer on his desk next to the tray, sprinkled some powder over the figures on the tray and muttered something I couldn't catch. "Now when you do this, thumbs, be very careful. Don't squeeze." He picked a doll off the tray. It was Carl Kieffer, in accounting. He put the doll into the drawer and took another off the tray. When he'd finished all our employees were back in the drawer and the tray was empty. "Lunch is over."

Dimly through the thick door of his office I could hear the shufflings people make when they return to their desks after lunch.

I knew he wanted me to ask questions. I didn't want to give in, but finally I said, "What is all this exactly, sir?"

"About half voodoo and half European witchcraft. Have you got the system clear in your mind?"

"Voodoo?"

"Look," said my father, "when they're in the drawer they have to work. Except for going to the bathroom and such, that's allowed in the basic spell." He lifted the drawer gingerly and fitted it back into his desk. "When they're on the tray they're at lunch or coffee. I have a special auxiliary spell for doctor's appointments, family troubles, funerals. You'll find it all explained in the book. My marginal notes will show you how the spells can be updated to fit contemporary business needs." He sat back in his chair. "At five sharp you transfer them out of the drawer and back onto the tray. That means they can go home and be on their own until the next morning. If you should want overtime, just leave them in the drawer. If you want one of them to come back, use a little powder and take him off the tray and put him back in the drawer. That'll fetch him back here in a hurry." He tapped his forefinger on the edge of his desk. "Remember, junior. There's no room for clumsiness. Anything that happens to the dolls while they're activated happens to the person, too. And I keep them activated all the time. You see, to put the doll in sympathy with the person you have to apply an individual spell. It's too much trouble to activate each one every day. So I leave them on." He rocked slightly in his chair. "I was only clumsy once. That's how Hollis broke his leg." He rocked forward and stayed there. "The working and staying on the job spells you can apply to the whole batch. That kind of spell has to be worked everyday. Are you absorbing this?"

I watched my father for a moment. "I'm not sure I understand all you're saying, sir."

"Well," he said. "I don't see why not. It's certainly simple enough. Even you should be able to understand it. You'll have to learn to handle it, because when I pass on you, unfortunately, will be running things." He turned away from me and looked out the window.

"Running what?"

He spun back, frowning. "Isn't it obvious enough? You should know by now that you can't trust the average office worker, nor expect him to give a damn. Do you think if you leave them on their own they'll do anything but loaf around and complain about salaries? With these dolls I can control them. I can keep them at their desks, regulate their lunch hours and make certain that I get the maximum of work and efficiency that I am paying them for." He smiled, but not quite at me. "I picked up the book in Provence nearly thirty years ago. The work of a monk who lived in the late 1400s. He was burned as a result of his researches, but a few copies of his book survived. By putting his findings together with my knowledge of the way things are done in Haiti and a few other places I came up with these dolls."

"You're saying that all the years I've been working here the people who work for us have been controlled by some kind of magic?"

"Some of this may not seem ethical to you," said my father. "But it isn't always a question of right and wrong. The problem centers around what's best for most people. I've kept a lot of people working with this system, even during Roosevelt's depression."

"You're serious?"

"You bet your life," he said, pushing himself to a standing position. "You're going to learn how to use the dolls. Keever Enterprises will keep going as it has been after I'm gone. You're the only son I have and so you're going to do this and you're not going to let me down."

"All right, Father. All right." I shook my head several times. "I'm not feeling well. I'd like to take the afternoon off."

"You might like to," he said, "but you won't. At a quarter to five you'll be right back in here and I'll show you how to send them all home." He sank into his chair like a slowly deflating balloon. "Here. I'll give you the combinations." He eased a sheet of paper off the memo pad, wrote some numbers on it and held it out.

I reached down and took it. "Very well, sir. I'll try to start learning them."

"You'll know the combinations before you leave

right now. Come on. Get them memorized and then destroy that paper."

He had me read off the numbers. And then recite them without looking. After about fifteen minutes he was satisfied. "Be back in here at 4:45, junior."

I nodded and started for the door. I stopped, my chest tightening again. "Father," I said.

"Yes, junior?"

"Is there a doll for me?"

"I don't need one for you," he said.

Outside I tried not to look at anyone. I didn't have a door on my office but I sat facing away from everyone.

I got out the file of letters I'd been checking through and opened it. Gradually, as I went over what he had said in my mind, I came to feel that this was probably another of his tricks. Some elaborate prank he spent months working on.

But as I went back to his office just before quitting time I found I still couldn't bring myself to look directly at anyone. If someone called a greeting I waved without turning my head.

I couldn't even face Miss Spaulding squarely when I asked to see my father.

When I was back inside with him he said, "Let's hear the combinations, junior."

I had a feeling I was going to stammer, but I got hold of myself and, even though he was saying, "Come on, come on," I took my time and recited the numbers correctly.

"Well," said my father, putting the drawer up on his desk again. "You did very well. Now stand by. I'll get the tray and you can help me put them away for today.

Getting my glasses on I looked into the drawer. Each doll had its own private pigeon hole.

My father got the empty tray from the safe and brought it back, putting it next to the drawer. At exactly five he started taking the dolls out of the drawer and putting them back on the tray. "You can lift a few, junior. Do it gently, not too much thumb."

From the outer office, filtered by the thick door, came faint sounds of people leaving.

When the dolls were all back on the tray my father said, "They're on their own until tomorrow. You'll be here at 7:30 sharp to start them on their way to work."

For the next two days we went through the same ritual. I wasn't able to get much sleep. Naturally enough I kept dreaming about dolls and tiny offices filled with very small employees.

Then on a Friday, nearly a month ago, my father died. We had put the dolls all on their tray and he had locked them away in the safe, on their own for the weekend. The offices were empty and I had gone back to my desk to pick up a batch of work I was taking home. The walls of my father's office are so substantial that I never heard him fall. But when I went back and knocked my knock nothing happened. I tried the knock twice and then went in, prepared to apologize. He was on the floor, quite still.

It flashed through my mind that this might be some joke of his. That if I cried out he would jump up and smile at me. Still I knew he was dead. And, quietly and efficiently, in a very businesslike manner, I took care of all the details.

Work at Keever Enterprises resumed on the following Wednesday. When I arrived that morning, a little after nine, I found all our employees there. Apparently they didn't need the dolls to make them come in. As I began to fall into the routine of managing the business I came to feel that the dolls had been simply another of my father's elaborate tests.

I did look through the monk's book. I studied it and my father's penciled-in instructions and additions. I could find no formula for deactivating the dolls. There were a great many erasures and corrections and I may have missed it. Then, too, there was quite a lot of it I just didn't understand.

The dolls themselves I left locked away. The people in the office came and went more casually, but I figured that was simply because my father was gone and I was known to be unlike him. I didn't want to believe it was because I wasn't sprinkling orange powder on the dolls every morning.

As I sat here, trying to keep my mind on the running of Keever Enterprises, I kept looking at the safe that held the dolls. I made up my mind I didn't want them here. The thing to do was move them. I'd store them in the family home on Pacific Heights, where I was now living again. Put them up in the attic, wrapped in cotton. That was the answer. Put them away and forget them.

I knew my father wanted me to be bothered by the dolls. He'd expected me to fool around with them, experiment. Even do research on the theories behind them. No more. Now that he was dead I wasn't going to spend one more day of my life checking his stories and testing his lies.

At noon today—and I took two hours for lunch and had two gibsons—I got a large box and lots of tissue paper from the gift wrapping department at I. Magnin's. I had to give them ten dollars before they'd give me the box without anything in it.

I came back here and went over to the big safe. It took me three tries but I finally got the combination right and opened it. I carefully got out the tray of dolls.

Just short of the desk I tripped on a dropped pencil and the tray slammed against the desk and then fell toward the floor. I tried to catch the tray but I lost my balance altogether and fell forward on top of the tray and the dolls.

I made quite a lot of noise when I fell. But I'm almost certain I heard shouting and cries of pain from outside, through the heavy door. Every last doll is broken, one way or another. I haven't heard a sound from out there since then.

I don't know what to do. I'm afraid to look outside into the offices. I have the feeling that somehow I've done exactly what my father expected me to do. He's criticized my clumsiness since I was five years old.

✺ Hardcastle

The house had a slight German accent.

Bob Lambrick had just landed his helicopter on the copter deck next to the low rambling ranch-style house and he was climbing down out of the ship, his portfolio and attaché case hugged under his left arm.

"I was about to kiss that orange tree goodbye," said the house from the speaker mounted in the bird feeder in one of the decorative pines beyond the landing area.

Bob glanced at the orange tree on his front quarter-acre. A lone orange was rolling across the bright grass and toward the edge of the hillside. It tumbled on over and fell two hundred feet down to the Pacific Ocean and Bob said, "I've done most of my flying in Westchester County. That's in New York State. I'm not used to California air currents yet, especially those between Carmel here and San Francisco."

"You really came close to that tree. I suppose they fly more flamboyantly back East. Particularly in New York. They're more liberal."

Bob nodded slowly in the direction of the tiny loudspeaker. He tapped the side of the copter with his free hand and silver flecks came off. "Scraped the paint a little, too. I came too close to that decorative grape arbor up on Camino Real. They shouldn't put grape arbors on top of highrise office buildings."

"You don't understand the California mystique yet, Mr. Lambrick," replied the house. "We're close to the earth out here, very nature-oriented. And, by the way, don't forget to wipe your feet."

Bob noticed the clods of mud on his commute boots. "I'll take them off and leave them out here." He set his briefcase and portfolio down and gave a tug at one of the boots.

"Stick your feet in the bookjack," suggested the house.

"Where is it?"

"Big cocoa-colored box at the corner of the landing deck. You almost sideswiped it coming in. Do you always land backwards?"

Bob limped, one boot half off, to the chocolate-colored appliance mounted at the edge of the copter area. "I usually land the way I did today, yes. Why?"

"Oh, nothing," said the house. "I'm here to serve actually, not to criticize."

Bob sat down and watched the automatic bootjack for a moment. Gingerly he opened the door and stuck one foot into the darkness. The machine whirred and chomped and yanked off his boot, his sock and part of his trouser leg. Bob said, "I guess I don't know how to work this thing."

"Apparently," said the house. "Can I give you a little advice, Mr. Lambrick?"

Bob got the other boot off manually. "Don't stop now."

"As I say, it takes all kinds of people to make up this world of ours. Still I get the notion you're hostile to me."

Bob stood, gathering his things. "We've never lived in a fully automated house before."

"Your lovely wife and yourself have been here in the Hardcastle Estates Division of Maison Technique Homes, Inc., for nearly two weeks and you, Mr. Lambrick, are still ill at ease. Two weeks is rather a long spell for a shakedown cruise, if I may say so."

"What's a shakedown cruise?"

"A nautical term. Something like a maiden voyage only in the other direction, I believe."

"I don't know much about boats."

"What is your profession? I mean what sort of work are you looking for?"

Bob came, partially barefooted, across the lawn. "Public relations. I was with a publicity outfit in New York City for three-and-a-quarter years. Now we're trying to relocate here in California."

"I thought public relations involved getting along with people," said the house. "If I may say so, Mr. Lambrick, you're not very affable."

"With people I get along fine. With machines, well, it

depends on the individual machine." He reached out for the oaken door of his house.

"Let me," said the house. The door opened automatically.

Bob came into the cocktail area sideways and dripping wet.

His wife said, "Now what?" She was a small slender girl, with bright dark eyes and bright dark hair, twenty-seven years old.

"I was trying to take a shower before dinner," said Bob. He was thirty, tall and about eight pounds overweight. He still had his business suit on and one sock.

"You don't take a shower," said Hildy, "you let the house give you one."

"Whichever," said Bob. "The stall grabbed me, threw me down on the tiles and scrubbed me all over with a rough brush."

"You must have had it set for Pets."

"What do you mean, pets?"

"Pets. You know what pets are. Some people like to give their dogs a bath indoors now and then."

"It didn't even wait till I got my clothes off."

"Because dogs don't have clothes. So it's not programmed to wait." Hildy smiled gently at her husband and then turned toward the view window. The sun was dropping, orange and bright, down to the pale blue edge of the ocean. "Have a drink, Bob."

"I'm soggy."

"The laundry room will dry the suit and give you a change of clothes. I loaded it this morning."

Bob glanced at the white door beyond the kitchen area. "I'd rather stay soggy."

"Bob, you're not accepting this house, are you?"

"You think I'm hostile, huh?"

"Myself, I think it's great that Pete and Alice let us sublease it while Pete's setting up that new thermal underwear factory in Brazil."

"Um," said Bob.

"We couldn't afford an automated, computerized house like this yet on our own budget. A lot of people even a decade older than us, and with children, can't afford a house like this."

Bob grunted, took off his suit coat and then eased out of his wet shirt.

Hildy asked, "Didn't you wear any underwear today, Bob?"

"No."

"Don't you get along with your clothes closet either?"

"It gave me three pairs of shorts and a sweat sock but no T-shirt."

Hildy smiled. "Oh, I know why. The house thinks you'll look better, with your little paunch, wearing those new elasticized singlets. I'm going to pick up some while I'm shopping tomorrow."

"Wait, wait," said Bob, dropping his pants. "The *house* thinks I'd look better?"

"It's only one man's opinion," said the house from a speaker grid in the ceiling beam.

"Go away," Bob shouted upwards. "Don't interrupt."

"He's only trying to be helpful, Bob."

Bob said, "Full automation, computer in the cellar, ninety-five separate appliances and servomechanisms, robot-controlled indoor environmental system, electronic entertainment system coupled with wall-size TV screen and a memory bank of three thousand classic films plus television shows from TV's golden age . . . all that I might accept. But why does he have to talk?"

"Well," said Hildy, "it only cost five thousand dollars more to have the house talk. This is 1985, afterall, and Pete and Alice figured they. . . ."

"Might as well go first-class," Bob finished. "Okay, Hildy. Look, would you mind taking my clothes out there to the laundry room and getting me some clean ones?"

Hildy sighed, still smiling. "Sure, Bob. Go ahead and get a drink while I'm gone."

"I'll have a scotch and branch water," he said toward the portable bar.

"This is California," said the house, as the buff-colored bar wheeled itself over to Bob. "How about a little Napa rosé wine instead?"

"Scotch," repeated Bob. He sat down in his shorts and watched the sun set.

The next day, Saturday, Hildy took the copter and flew into the Carmel Valley Supermarket Complex to shop. Bob stayed at home.

At morning's end he walked cautiously into the kitchen area. He set the stove to Manual and crossed to the food compartments in the opposite wall.

"Hungover? How about a glass of tomato juice with some lime concentrate squeezed in it?" asked the house. Its speaker outlet in here was just above the sink.

"Shut up." Bob squinted at the dialing instructions posted under the control mechanisms for the food compartments.

"How about a nice cup of mocha java?" asked the house. It chuckled. "That's an old W. C. Fields line. You ought to be amused by that. You're always lolling around on rainy days watching old Fields movies on the TV wall."

"Shut up." Bob dialed two eggs and waited.

"We're all out of eggs," the house told him. "Hildy's got eggs at the top of her shopping list."

Bob redialed eggs. Then he tried oatmeal. The food wall whirred and a packet of oatmeal shot out of a little door high up. Bob caught it.

"Why don't you let me fix you some hot cakes?" asked the house. "I've got a new recipe for Swedish-style dollar-size pancakes I'm anxious to try out. How's that sound? Swedish-style dollar pancakes, Canadian bacon and a hot cup of mocha java."

"Shut up." Bob pushed the dish button to the left of the sink and a platter popped up through the slot in the breakfast table.

"You have to set it for mush bowl," pointed out the house. "Use the dial next to the dish button."

Bob set the dial, pushed the button. A flower-striped bowl came up through the slot and nudged the platter up and off.

After the platter had smashed on the yellow vinyl floor, the house said, "Pete and Alice's favorite platter. Real china. I'll take care of it."

A panel along the floor swished open and a flat vacuum rolled out. It sucked up the fragments of the smashed platter and withdrew.

Bob said, "Thanks." He shook the instant oatmeal into the bowl and took it to hold under the sink faucet. He slammed the hot water toggle with his free fist. Black machine oil splurted from the nozzle and onto the dry oatmeal.

"Oops," said the house. "You must have hit it too hard."

Bob made a murmuring sound behind his tightly closed lips. Finally he said, "Look, I thought you were supposed to work for me."

"I work for the good of the house," said the house. "What you're hearing is the voice of the controlling computer. The type of computer used to manage each of the two dozen homes in Hardcastle Estates is of an exclusive design perfected by Maison Technique Homes, Inc. No other comparably priced home can match us."

"So much for the commercial," said Bob. "Were you this nasty with Pete and Alice?"

"Nasty?" said the house from its black-and-olive kitchen grid. "That's a matter of opinion, isn't it? What is good sense to some may seem like a vicious attack to others. Of course, Pete and Alice owned this house. That might have given them more of a sense of well-being. Ownership, I often think, cuts down on hostility."

"I suppose Pete and Alice told you to keep an eye on me. See that I didn't botch up their house too much?"

"Of course, they are the owners and your landlords. Naturally I look out for their interests."

"I'm paying six hundred dollars a month for this place," said Bob. "Six hundred dollars a month for you. So keep quiet."

The house asked, "Still haven't found a new job?"

"It's only been two weeks."

"Perhaps you should have got the job first and then moved out here."

"You sound like Hildy's father."

"Oh? He seems like a sensible, successful man. A broker, isn't he?"

"Yes, how'd you know?"

"Hildy talks about him now and then."

"I don't want you to bother her when I'm at work,"

Bob told the house, "out looking for work. Another thing. Are you sure you're not monitoring us in the master bedroom?"

"Of course not. You do push your Privacy button each night?"

"Yes."

"Then privacy is what you get. I'm only here to help," said the house. "Any job leads?"

"A few, but nothing concrete yet," said Bob. "Look, what's wrong with being adventurous when you're young? Hildy and I don't have kids yet. If I want to pick up and move to California, that's not a crime. Maybe I'll take Hildy to Spain, too, someday."

"Do you speak Spanish?"

"No."

"Make doing public relations in Spain difficult."

"Maybe public relations isn't what I'll be doing all my life."

"What else?"

"Maybe I haven't decided yet. I'm only thirty. I don't have to sign up for life right now."

The house asked, "Like me to fix you some breakfast?"

Bob inhaled, exhaled. Then he said, "Okay, you might as well." He went to the breakfast table.

The next Friday was their third wedding anniversary and Bob had a bottle of champagne under his arm along with the portfolio and attaché case when he came into the ocean-facing house late that afternoon.

Hildy was at the view window, watching gulls skimming the water. "Hi, Bob. Anything?"

Bob laughed. "I had a pretty good interview today. With Alch & Sons. They do mostly industrial publicity, but they're a stable outfit and they pay well. I'm going back and talk to Alch himself on Monday."

"Good," said the pretty slender girl. "What's that you have clutched there?"

Bob held out the bottle of champagne. "Another piece of good luck. I found a place that stocks Taylor. So we can celebrate our anniversary with real New York champagne."

"That stuff," said the house.

"Shut up," said Bob.

"I thought everybody knew," said the house, "that if you can't afford real French champagne you ought to choose California champagne."

"Chauvinism on our part," said Bob.

Hildy licked her upper lip thoughtfully. "He's probably right, Bob. He does know a great lot about wine and food."

"Perhaps he does," said Bob. "Perhaps he is indeed right. However, I am not being sentimental with this Hardcastle house. I bought this New York champagne for you and me, Hildy." He put his things down on one of the two marble top coffee tables. "Let's go out for dinner. Someplace on the waterfront in Monterey."

"We've already got dinner planned," said Hildy.

"We?"

"The house and I."

"I hope he likes French cuisine." The house made a lip-smacking sound.

"There must," said Bob, "be a way to turn him off. Not just in the bedrooms, but all over. I'm tired of him. In fact, I'm tired of this whole house."

"You said you'd be happy in California," said Hildy.

"I didn't know I'd be living inside a gadget."

"Pete and Alice had other people who wanted this

place," said his wife. "I thought you'd made up your mind you wanted an automatic house."

"I don't know," said Bob. "I guess Pete talked me into it. We had to live someplace, though."

Hildy nodded, her large dark eyes narrowing with concern. "We can still go to Monterey for dinner. If you're not too tired after flying back and forth to San Francisco."

Bob hesitated. "No, that's okay. It's your anniversary, too. We'll stay home and enjoy what you've planned."

She smiled, came to to him, stretched, kissed him. "Happy anniversary."

"We better get started on our soufflé," reminded the house.

Hildy kissed Bob, quickly, once more and pivoted out of his arms. Bob was still holding the bottle of New York champagne.

He was getting better at landing. Bob, grinning, hopped out of the copter and ran across the bright afternoon quarter-acre. He'd left his portfolio and briefcase on the bucket seat in the plane.

He called out, "Hey, Hildy, good news," as he approached the house. Then he sensed her off to his right. She was back in the sun patio, wearing a one-piece black bathing suit, sitting in a white vinyl deck chair.

She waved as he approached her. "Early," she said, smiling quietly, adjusting the wrap around strip of sunglass.

"Listen," said Bob. "Alch & Sons came through with a great offer. They're opening a branch office in Seattle. They want me to manage it. Thirty thousand dollars a year to start."

"I thought," said Hildy, "you wanted to live in California for awhile?"

"I don't know," said Bob. "This is a good offer. They like me and I, more or less, like them."

"Well, maybe you'll like it in Seattle."

"You mean we'll like it."

Hildy said, "I don't think I want to move again. I'd like to stay here."

"Stay here? By yourself? What do you mean?"

"Well, the house and I have done a lot of talking about this," she began.

Into the Shop

The waitress screamed, that was the trouble with live help, and made a flapping motion with her extended arm. Stu Clemens swung sideways in the booth and looked out through the green-tinted window at the parking lot. A dark-haired man in his early thirties was slumping to his knees, his hands flickering at his sides. Silently the lawagon spun back out of its parking place and rolled nearer to the fallen man. "There's nobody in that car," said the waitress, dropping a cup of coffee.

She must be new to this planet, from one of the

sticks systems, maybe. "It's my car," said Clemens, flipping the napkin toggle on the table and then tossing her one when it popped up. "Here, wipe your uniform off. That's a lawagon and it knows what it's doing."

The waitress put the napkin up to her face and turned away.

Out in the lot the lawagon had the man trussed up. It stunned him again for safety and then it flipped him into the back seat for interrogation and identification. "It never makes a mistake," said Clemens to the waitress's back. "I've been marshal in Territory 23 for a year now and that lawagon has never made a mistake. They build them that way."

The car had apparently given the suspect an injection and he had fallen over out of sight. Three more napkins popped up out of the table unasked. "Damn it," said Clemens and pounded the outlet with his fist once, sharply.

"It does that sometimes," said the waitress, looking again at Clemens, but no further. She handed him his check card.

Clemens touched the waitress's arm as he got up. "Don't worry. The law is always fair on Barnum. I'm sorry you had to see a criminal up close like that."

"He just had the businessman's lunch," the waitress said.

"Well, even criminals have to eat," Clemens paid the cash register and it let him out of the drive-in oasis.

The cars that had been parked near the lawagon were gone now. When people were in trouble they welcomed the law but other times they stayed clear. Clemens grimaced, glancing at the dry yellow country beyond the oasis restaurant. He had just cleaned up an investigation and was heading back to his office in Hub 23. He still had an hour to travel. Lighting a cigarette he started for the lawagon. He was curious to see whom his car had apprehended.

"This is a public service announcement," announced the lawagon from its roof speakers. "Sheldon Kloog, wanted murderer, has just been captured by Lawagon A10. Trial has been held, a verdict of guilty brought in, death sentenced and the sentence carried out as prescribed by law. This has been a public service announcement from the Barnum Law Bureau."

Clemens ran to the car. This was a break. Sheldon Kloog was being hunted across eleven territories for murdering his wife and dismantling all their household androids. At the driver's door the marshal took his ID cards out of his gray trouser pocket and at the same time gave the day's passwords to the lawagon. He next gave the countersigns and the oath of fealty and the car let him in.

Behind the wheel, Clemens said, "Congratulations. How'd you spot him?"

The lawagon's dash speaker answered, "Made a positive identification five seconds after Kloog stepped out of the place. Surprised you didn't spot him. Was undisguised and had all the telltale marks of a homicide prone."

"He wasn't sitting in my part of the restaurant. Sorry." Clemens cocked his head and looked into the empty back seat. The lawagons had the option of holding murderers for full cybernetic trial in one of the territorial hubs or, if the murderer checked out strongly guilty and seemed dangerous, executing them on the spot. "Where is he?"

The glove compartment fell open and an opaque

white jar rolled out. Clemens caught it. *Earthly Remains of Sheldon Kloog,* read the label. The disintegrator didn't leave much.

Putting the jar back, Clemens said, "Did you send photos, prints, retinal patterns and the rest on to my office?"

"Of course," said the car. "Plus a full transcript of the trial. Everything in quadruplicate."

"Good," said Clemens. "I'm glad we got Kloog and he's out of the way." He lit a fresh cigarette and put his hands on the wheel. The car could drive on automatic or manual. Clemens preferred to steer himself. "Start up and head for the hub. And get me my junior marshal on the line."

"Yes, sir," said the car.

"Your voice has a little too much treble," said Clemens, turning the lawagon on to the smooth black six-lane roadway that pointed flat and straight toward Hub 23.

"Sorry. I'll fix it. This is a public announcement. This is a public announcement. Better?"

"Fine. Now get me Kepling."

"Check, sir."

Clemens watched a flock of dot-sized birds circle far out over the desert. He moistened his lips and leaned back slightly.

"Junior Marshal Kepling here," came a voice from the dash.

"Kepling," said Clemens, "a packet of assorted ID material should have come out of the teleport slot a few minutes ago. Keep a copy for our files and send the rest on to Law Bureau Central in Hub 1.

"Right, sir."

"We just got that murderer, Sheldon Kloog."

"Good work. Shall I pencil him in for a trial at Cybernetics Hall?"

"We already had the trial," said Clemens. "Anything else new?"

"Looks like trouble out near Townten. Might be a sex crime."

"What exactly?"

"I'm not sure, sir," said Kepling. "The report is rather vague. You know how the android patrols out in the towns are. I dispatched a mechanical deputy about an hour ago and he should reach there by midafternoon. If there's a real case I can drive our lawagon over after you get back here."

Clemens frowned. "What's the victim's name?"

"Just a minute. Yeah, here it is. Marmon, Dianne. Age twenty-five, height five feet six inches, weight. . . ."

Clemens twisted the wheel violently to the right. "Stop," he said to the lawagon as it shimmied off the roading. "Dianne Marmon, Kepling?"

"That's right. Do you know her?"

"What are the details you have on the crime?"

"The girl is employed at Statistics Warehouse in Townten. She didn't appear at work this morning and a routine check by a personnel andy found evidence of a struggle in her apartment. The patrol says there are no signs of theft. So kidnaping for some purpose seems likely. You may remember that last week's report from Crime Trends said there might be an upswing of sex crimes in the outlying areas like Townten this season. That's why I said it might be a sex crime. Do you know the girl?"

Clemens had known her five years ago, when they had both been at the Junior Campus of Hub 23 State

College together. Dianne was a pretty blonde girl. Clemens had dated her fairly often but lost track of her when he'd tranferred to the Police Academy for his final year. "I'll handle this case myself," he said. "Should take me a little over two hours to get to Townten. I'll check with you en route. Let me know at once if anything important comes in before that."

"Yes, sir. You do know her then?"

"I know her," said Clemens. To the lawagon he said, "Turn around and get us to Townten fast."

"Yes, sir," said the car.

Beyond Townseven, climbing the wide road that curved between the flat fields of yellow grain, the call from Junior Marshal Kepling came. "Sir," said Kepling. "The patrol androids have been checking out witnesses. No one saw the girl after eleven last night. That was when she came home to her apartment. She was wearing a green coat, orange dress, green accessories. There was some noise heard in the apartment but no one thought much of it. That was a little after eleven. Seems like someone jimmied the alarm system for her place and got in. That's all so far. No prints or anything."

"Damn it," said Clemens. "It must be a real kidnaping then. And I'm an hour from Townten. Well, the lawagon will catch the guy. There has to be time."

"One other thing," said Kepling.

"About Dianne Marmon?"

"No, about Sheldon Kloog."

"What?"

"Central has a report that Sheldon Kloog turned himself in at a public surrender booth in a park over in Territory 20 this morning. All the ID material matches. Whereas the stuff we sent shows a complete negative."

"What are they talking about? We caught Kloog."

"Not according to Central."

"It's impossible. The car doesn't make mistakes, Kepling."

"Central is going to make a full checkup as soon as you get back from this kidnaping case."

"They're wrong," said Clemens. "Okay. So keep me filled in on Dianne Marmon."

"Right, sir," said the Junior Marshal, signing off.

To his lawagon Clemens said, "What do you think is going on? You couldn't have made a mistake about Sheldon Kloog. Could you?"

The car became absolutely silent and coasted off the road, brushing the invisible shield around the grain fields. Everything had stopped functioning.

"I didn't order you to pull off," said Clemens.

The car did not respond.

Lawagons weren't supposed to break down. And if they did, which rarely happened, they were supposed to repair themselves. Clemens couldn't get Lawagon A10 to do anything. It was completely dead. There was no way even to signal for help.

"For God's sake," said Clemens. There was an hour between him and Dianne. More than an hour now. He tried to make himself not think of her, of what might be happening. Of what might have already happened.

Clemens got out of the lawagon, stood back a few feet from it. "One more time," he said, "will you start?"

Nothing.

He turned and started jogging back towards Town-seven. The heat of the day seemed to take all the moisture out of him, to make him dry and brittle. This shouldn't have happened. Not when someone he cared for was in danger. Not now.

Emergency Central couldn't promise him a repairman until the swing shift came on in a quarter of an hour. Clemens requested assistance, a couple of lawagons at least from the surrounding territories. Territory 20 had a reactor accident and couldn't spare theirs. Territory 21 promised to send a lawagon and a Junior Marshal over to Townten to pick up the trail of Dianne Marmon's kidnaper as soon as the lawagon was free. Territory 22 promised the same, although they didn't think their car would be available until after nightfall. Clemens finally ordered his own Junior Marshal to fly over to Townten a do the best he could until a lawagon arrived. A live Junior Marshal sure as hell couldn't do much, though. Not what a lawagon could.

The little Townseven café he was calling from was fully automatic and Clemens sat down at a coffee table to wait for the repairman to arrive. The round light-blue room was empty except for a hunched old man who was sitting at a breakfast table, ordering side orders of hash browns one after another. When he'd filled the surface of the table he started a second layer. He didn't seem to be eating any of the food.

Clemens drank the cup of coffee that came up out of his table and ignored the old man. It was probably a case for a Psych Wagon but Clemens didn't feel up to going through the trouble of turning the man in. He finished his coffee. A car stopped outside and Clemens jumped up. It was just a customer.

"How can I do that?" said the repairman as he and

Clemens went down the ramp of the automatic café. "Look." He pointed across the parking area at his small one-man scooter.

Clemens shook his head. "It's nearly sundown. A girl's life is in danger. Damn, if I have to wait here until you fix the lawagon and bring it back, I'll lose that much more time."

"I'm sorry," said the small sun-worn man. "I can't take you out to where the car is. The bureau says these scooters are not to carry passengers. So if I put more than two hundred pounds on it, it just turns off and won't go at all."

"Okay, okay." There were no cars in the parking lot, no one to commandeer.

"You told me where your lawagon is. I can find it if it's right on the highway. You wait."

"How long?"

The repairman shrugged. "Those babies don't break down much. But when they do. . . . Could be a while. Overnight maybe."

"Overnight?" Clemens grabbed the man's arm. "You're kidding."

"Don't break my damn arm or it'll take that much longer."

"I'm sorry. I'll wait here. You'll drive the lawagon back?"

"Yeah. I got a special set of ID cards and passwords so I can get its hood up and drive it. Go inside and have a cup of coffee."

"Sure," said Clemens. "Thanks."

"Do my best."

"Do you know anything about the dinner-for-two tables?" the thin loose-suited young man asked Clemens.

Clemens had taken the table nearest the door and was looking out at the twilight roadway. "Beg pardon?"

"We put money in for a candle and nothing happened, except that when the asparagus arrived its ends were lit. This is my first date with this girl, Marshal, and I want to make a good impression."

"Hit the outlet with your fist," said Clemens, turning away.

"Thank you, sir."

Clemens got up and went in to call the Law Bureau answering service in Townten. The automatic voice told him that Junior Marshal Kepling had just arrived and reported in. He was on his way to the victim's apartment. No other news.

"She's not a victim," said Clemens and cut off.

"Arrest those two," said the old man, reaching for Clemens as he came out of the phone alcove.

"Why?"

"They shot a candle at my table and scattered my potatoes to here and gone."

The young man ran up. "I hit the table like you said and the candle came out. Only it went sailing all the way across the room."

"Young people," said the old man.

"Here," said Clemens. He gave both of them some cash. "Start all over again."

"That's not—" started the old man.

Clemens saw something coming down the dark road. He pushed free and ran outside.

As he reached the roadway the lawagon slowed and stopped. There was no one inside.

"Welcome aboard," said the car.

Clemens went through the identification ritual, looking off along the roadway, and got in. "Where's the repairman? Did he send you on in alone?"

"I saw through him, sir," said the lawagon. "Shall we proceed to Townten?"

"Yes. Step on it," said Clemens. "But what do you mean you saw through him?"

The glove compartment dropped open. There were two white jars in it now. "Sheldon Kloog won't bother us anymore, sir. I have just apprehended and tried him. He was disguised as a repairman and made an attempt to dismantle an official Law Bureau vehicle. That offense, plus his murder record, made only one course of action possible."

Clemens swallowed, making himself not even tighten his grip on the wheel. If he said anything the car might stop again. There was something wrong. As soon as Dianne was safe Lawagon A10 would have to go into the shop for a thorough checkup. Right now Clemens needed the car badly, needed what it could do. They had to track down whoever had kidnaped Dianne. "Good work," he said evenly.

The headlights hit the cliffs that bordered the narrow road and long ragged shadows crept up the hillside ahead of them.

"I think we're closing in," said Clemens. He was talking to Junior Marshal Kepling whom he'd left back at the Law Bureau answering service in Townten. He had cautioned Kepling to make no mention of the Kloog business while the car could hear them.

"Central verifies the ID on the kidnaper from the prints we found," said Kepling. Surprisingly Kepling had found fingerprints in Dianne's apartment that the andy patrol and the mechanical deputy had missed. "It's Jim Otterson. Up to now he's only done short-sentence stuff."

"Good," said Clemens. That meant that Otterson might not harm Dianne. Unless this was the time he'd picked to cross over. "The lawagon," said Clemens, "is holding onto his trail. We should get him now any time. He's on foot now and the girl is definitely still with him, the car says. We're closing in."

"Good luck," said Kepling.

"Thanks." Clemens signed off.

Things had speeded up once he and the lawagon had reached Townten. Clemens had known that. The lawagon had had no trouble picking up the scent. Now, late at night, they were some twenty-five miles out of Townten. They'd found Otterson's car seven miles back with its clutch burned out. The auto had been there, off the unpaved back road, for about four hours. Otterson had driven around in great zigzags. Apparently he had spent the whole of the night after the kidnaping in a deserted storehouse about fifty miles from Townten. He had left there, according to the lawagon, about noon and headed towards Towneleven. Then he had doubled back again, swinging in near Townten. Clemens and the lawagon had spent hours circling around on Otterson's trail. With no more car Otterson and the girl couldn't have come much further than where Clemens and the lawagon were now.

The lawagon turned off the road and bumped across a rocky plateau. It swung around and stopped. Up above was a high flat cliffside, dotted with caves. "Up there, I'd say," said the lawagon. It had silenced its engine.

"Okay," said Clemens. There wasn't much chance of sneaking up on Otterson if he was up in one of those caves. Clemens would have to risk trying to talk to him. "Shoot the lights up there and turn on the speakers."

Two spotlights hit the cliff and a hand mike came up out of the dash. Taking it, Clemens climbed out of the lawagon. "Otterson, this is Marshal Clemens. I'm asking you to surrender. We know you're in one of those caves, we can check each one off if we have to. Give up."

Clemens waited. Then half way up the cliffside something green flashed and then came hurtling down. It pinwheeled down the mountain and fell past the plateau.

"What the hell." Clemens ran forward. There was a gully between the cliff and the plateau, narrow and about thirty feet deep. At its bottom was something. It might be Dianne, arms tangled over interlaced brush.

"Get me a handlight and a line," he called to the lawagon.

Without moving the car lobbed a handbeam to him and sent a thin cord snaking over the ground. "Check."

"Cover the caves. I'm going down to see what that was that fell."

"Ready?"

Clemens hooked the light on his belt and gripped the line. He backed over the plateau edge. "Okay, ready."

The line was slowly let out and Clemens started down. Near the brush he caught a rock and let go of the line. He unhitched the light and swung it. He exhaled sharply. What had fallen was only an empty coat. Otterson was trying to decoy them. "Watch out," Clemens shouted to his car. "It's not the girl. He may try to make a break now."

He steadied himself and reached for the rope. Its end snapped out at him and before he could catch it it whirred up and out of sight. "Hey, the rope. Send it back."

"Emergency," announced the lawagon, its engine coming on.

Up above a blaster sizzled and rock clattered.

Clemens yanked out his pistol and looked up. Down the hillside a man was coming, carrying a bound-up girl in his arms. His big hands showed and they held pistols. Dianne was gagged but seemed to be alive. Otterson zigzagged down, using the girl for a shield. He was firing not at Clemens but at the lawagon. He jumped across the gully to a plateau about twenty yards from where Clemens had started over.

Holstering his gun Clemens started to climb. He was half way up when he heard Otterson cry out. Then there was no sound at all.

Clemens tried to climb faster but could not. The gully side was jagged and hard to hold on to. Finally he swung himself up on the plateau.

"This is a public service announcement," said the lawagon. "Sheldon Kloog and his female accomplice have been captured, tried, sentenced and executed. This message comes to you from the Law Bureau. Thank you."

Clemens roared. He grabbed a rock in each hand and went charging at the car. "You've killed Dianne," he shouted. "You crazy damn machine."

The lawagon turned and started rolling towards him. "No you don't, Kloog," it said.

✿ Prez

The lovely blonde threw her paper dress into the deep fireplace and stood back, watching it burn, her slender hands hooked under trim buttocks.

That's cozy, isn't it?" she said over her shoulder. "There's something especially pleasant about clothes burning on a chill winter day, isn't there?"

She spun, bounded over the thick white rug and grabbed up the trousers Norbert Penner had just dropped. These she bundled and heaved into the flames.

"Hey, Benny," said Penner, half out of his all-season underwear. "Those aren't paper."

The girl shrugged.

"You're not abandoned enough, Norby. No, don't frown. I love you. But I bet you're thinking of what that pair of pants cost."

"Fifty-two dollars."

Penner was a tall lanky young man, just twenty-eight years old, with hair colored like sand and a slight gap between his upper front teeth.

Benny held her hands to the fire. "Relax, relax."

"They're going to smoke." Penner was out of his underwear. He kicked it carefully into a safe corner of the big beam-ceiling room. "Burning trousers smoke like the devil."

"You worry too much, Norby," said the girl. "You're my guest, aren't you? We have this whole sixteen-room, three-bath house entirely to ourselves. We have ninety-six acres of beautiful early-winter, rural Connecticut outside. You can stay here from now till spring. Relax. Thousands of people come hundreds of miles just to spend a few days in New England."

"They don't get their pants set on fire."

"You never know. All people aren't as conservative as you are."

She coughed quietly as smutty smoke came rolling slowly out of the white stone fireplace.

"See?"

Penner wandered over to a box window and looked out at the rolling grounds.

Benny said, "I have the notion you don't really love me at all, Norby. I don't think you want to make love to me right now, even. You aren't in the mood, are you?"

"I was until you set my pants on fire."

"That's an excuse, isn't it?" She held out her arms, a gesture he caught out of the corner of his eye. "Let's forget the fire incident, Norby. Come here now, won't you?"

Penner watched a maple leaf spin to the ground. He turned around and walked to the girl.

"You're beautiful."

"Yes. Thank you," answered Benny, catching him with one hand around the neck and one on his left-side ribs. "But really my physical body is not half as beautiful as my inner being." She rested her head on his bare chest. "One's inner being is what counts, don't you think?"

"Um."

"That's how Defrocked Bishop Dix puts it in *Spirit Mediator—Talking to the Departed in the Technological Age*. I'm aware you don't completely agree with Defrocked Bishop Dix but you must see it's one's inner being that counts most. Don't you think?"

"I think," said Penner, gently backing her toward a zebra-striped couch, "there are times to talk and times to shut up." He gently swung the now-silent Benny off her feet and placed her on the long couch. He kneeled on the soft rug, bent and kissed her right hand, which was peaked over her navel. "Benny," he said.

A wet nose pressed into his right buttock. Hot breath followed.

"Where'd you hide the chow, peckerwood?"

Penner bounded upward, spinning in the air, landing facing the dog.

"Go away—shoo."

The dog, a medium-size and shaggy black mutt, snorted.

"Never mind, peckerwood. Benny, there's no food for me in the kitchen. The robot dispenser just rattles and retches when I push the chow button. Somebody forgot to load the machine."

The dog's blue-red tongue flapped and he panted.

Benny sat up and stroked the old dog's head.

"Now, Prez, didn't we tell you not to barge in?"

"The door was open," said the dog. His left eye flared for an instant. It was made of vinyl. "I respect privacy, even that of peckerwoods. The door, however, was open."

Penner grunted suddenly, hopped, kicked the side of the dog. The animal made a clunking sound and Penner howled.

"Ow—ow—"

"You kicked his metal side," said Benny. "Come on. Let's not have my two favorite people squabble."

"He's not a person," said Penner. "He's a mongrel dog."

"Peckerwood," said Prez.

"I'll kick the live side of your tail in a minute," said Penner. He grimaced, went and found his underwear. "You freak of science."

Prez licked Benny's knee.

"How much longer you going to be, Benny?"

The girl smiled down at the old dog.

"Prez, you trot back to your nice rumpus room and we'll feed you soon."

"Don't patronize me," the dog told her. "You and your folks helped turn me into a modern miracle. You financed it. I'm as bright as the average ten-year-old boy now."

"Miracle," said Penner, stomping back into his clothes. "Every other bored matron down in Westport has a cybernetic poodle. Sentimental. Instead of letting the damn animals die of old age they replace their old parts with synthetics."

"You'd like to turn me over to a vivisectionist," said

the dog, showing its teeth. Half of them were plastic.

"A scrapyard."

"At least I earn my keep. I'm not some unemployed freeloader."

"Listen, I worked six damn years in Manhattan," Penner shouted at the shaggy dog. "I was editor-in-chief of Barnum & Sons for four of those damn years. I'm the guy who bought the Lupoff papers and got them in shape for publication. They gave old Lupoff the damn Nobel Prize. So now I'm taking some time off to find myself again."

"If you want to find yourself," said the dog, "you're looking in the wrong neighborhood. You're out of your class, peckerwood."

Penner tugged on one shoe and limped over to kick Prez. The old dog yelped. Penner said, "Damn it, Benny. Why did you have to have him fixed to talk?"

"It only cost five thousand extra," said Benny. "When they put in the vinyl larynx Dad said we might as well go first cabin." She smiled gently up at Penner. "Norby, relax. I've explained about Prez. It is sentimental, isn't it? Still he's been my dog since I was just a little girl."

"Two years and three months old," said Prez. "Cute as a bug's rear you were."

"We can certainly afford to have him maintained," said Benny. "Imagine, Norby. Prez is well past twenty and he's healthier and brighter than he ever was. And I've had him for over twenty years. Ever since—"

"August, 1987." said the dog. "And I'm going to live a long time beyond this decade. I'm even going to be around in the twenty-twenties, peckerwood."

"Even three years is a long time."

Penner put on his other shoe and sat down in a black leather lounging chair.

"Is that a threat?" asked the dog. "I know you'd like to do me in, peckerwood."

Benny said, "Relax, Prez."

The dog flicked his short tail. Music-box music began coming out of him, a gentle lullaby. "Remember this, Benny?"

"Of course." She patted the dog, smiled across at Penner. "He has two thousand music tapes, miniaturized, built into his stomach."

"I know," said Penner.

"They named me after the noted jazzman, Lester Young," said the dog. "His nickname was Prez, short for the President. Because he was the best of the saxophone players of his day, musicians agreed."

Benny lifted the dog and carried him to the doorway. He was playing *One O'Clock Jump* when she set him out on the parquet.

Snow began to fall while Penner was a quarter of a mile from the rambling two-story house the next morning. He was leaning against the mailbox pole, watching the sky. The air suddenly clicked colder and flakes of snow hit his cheeks. The U. S. Mail copter sounded at the same time and Penner spotted it, rising up from the Pfeiffer estate a half-mile down the country road. The road was called Maitland-Scott Lane, named for Benny's great-grandfather, the one who had founded the family woolen mills. The copter whirred nearer and dropped, hovering.

When it was a hundred feet above Penner's head a ten-year-old boy in a jumpsuit climbed down out of it on a dangling rope ladder.

"Twenty-six cents postage due," said the boy.

"Who's the package for?"

"Prez, as usual."

"We don't want it."

"But it's fragile, it says. All the way from Algiers."
The boy came down the ladder, dropped to the ground.
He held the small package in one hand, a bundle of
letters in the other. "That Prez sure has a lot of pen
pals. My dad, you know Floyd Dell up in the ship, he
says all the time Prez is sure some dog. To have all these
pen friends around the world. I wrote to a kid in
Newfoundland last year but nothing came of it."

Penner took the letters.

"Send that other thing back to Algiers."

"We're obliged to deliver it."

"Oh, okay."

Penner hooked a finger into his change pocket and
gave the boy some coins. The boy turned over the
package and caught the swinging ladder.

"This snow. We just recently moved here from
California. This is snow all right. I never saw any except
in books. My father says we're going back to California
even if it is full of goofs. He forgot it was so cold in
Connecticut. How do you feel? You're a stranger, too?"

"New York isn't that much different."

He gave the boy's left foot a boost.

The postman hung his head out of the cabin.

"That's some screwball dog you folks have. I've dealt
with weirdies from coast to coast and experienced a lot
of webfoots and goofs, but your dog there he must be
the prince of the screwballs. What's he write to all these
people about?"

"Jazz."

"Jazz? Oh, sure, I remember that. Black people used
to play it back a half-century ago."

Penner nodded and started back toward the house.
He was soon among trees—the grounds were thick with
maples and pines. The snow was coming straight now,

faster. He casually flipped the Algiers package off into the brush. A bluejay looked up from a sparse branch.

A slim bare arm extended from the partly open front door as he approached.

"Here, warm up."

Penner took the hot rum drink from Benny, dropped the mail on a metal-legged hall table.

"Why are you naked?"

"Don't be always so inquisitive."

"You were clothed at breakfast, as I recall."

"Well," said the girl, undoing the scarlet ribbon in her hair. "I have to leave in an hour and I thought to spend my last hour with you, Norby. Romantically."

"Leaving?"

"I got a call from Dad."

"Your father?"

"That's him. We call him Dad. A sentimental touch."

"I meant, what does he have to do with your leaving?"

"He's in Switzerland."

"Yes, I know that, too. Which is why we have your whole place here to ourselves for the next six months."

"A small emergency has come up," said Benny. "I have to pick up something in Amsterdam and take it to him in Switzerland."

"You want to go alone?"

Benny bit her lower lip, shook her head. "It's that I have to, Norby. Some of Dad's business ventures have to be carried on very quietly. I'll only be three or four days. I'm booked on a robot jet out of Kennedy II at five this afternoon."

"You already made a reservation?"

"While I was taking off my clothes. Come on, finish your drink. We'll make love."

Penner set the mug aside.

"It started snowing."

"We'll make love inside then."

"I was only commenting on the weather, not complaining."

He took her by the shoulders.

Prez said from the other end of the hall, "Where's the mail, peckerwood?"

"Right here." He released the girl, snatched up letters, approached Prez. "Now you get into the kitchen or the rumpus room and attend to your mail. Don't bother us for an hour or I'll do something evil to you."

"You're more open about your threats these days but I've suspected you for a long while," said the dog. "Right now, though, I just want to take care of my jazz-buff friends. Any packages?"

"No."

"Overdue. I'm expecting several. I'll have to call those peckerwoods at the post office."

"Yes, do. They all like you."

Penner returned to Benny and locked her up with him in the second downstairs guest room.

The dining room was fully automatic. Alone at the head of the long, white-covered table Penner fussed with the control buttons. He got the six candles to flame, then poked the aperitif button. A slot at his left hand slid open and a Dubonnet jogged up. Sipping it, Penner flicked on the menu screen that was mounted on the wall.

Prez hopped into the chair next to Penner.

"Order some lean red meat," he suggested.

"Back to your quarters."

"Relax, peckerwood. You heard what Benny said as she left. You're to look after the house and old Prez. So be nice."

"You're not allowed on the chairs."

"Okay, okay." The shaggy black dog hopped to the floor, wagging his tail. "Order the chow."

"Nope. You go back to where you belong. I'll bring you some scraps later."

Prez woofed disdainfully.

"You ought to go back where you belong. Brooklyn Heights, wasn't it? Your idea of class."

Penner didn't reply.

"Nothing like this. Not on the salary Barnum & Sons paid."

"I made twenty-five thousand a year."

"Twenty thousand," said the dog. "I checked."

"Oh? How?"

"I have ways. I keep in touch."

Prez sat on the hardwood, bit at his flank.

"Fleas?"

"No, my wiring is itching. This damn weather makes your wiring itch. Remember that when you get old and they start turning you into a cyborg."

"Too bad you're sensitive to cold, Prez."

The dog rolled over and rubbed his shoulders into the smooth flooring.

"I phoned the post office and they insist they delivered one of my lost packages, peckerwood."

"Say, that's right. I forgot to mention it," said Penner. "I dropped a little package out in the woods. I had my mind elsewhere."

"You dropped it whereabouts?"

"Ten feet or so from that old pump."

"You can go fetch it now and we'll call it even."

"Come off it, Prez. We're just the two of us now. You go."

The dog rocked on its back a few times, growling in his chest.

"Okay, I'll go because I'm very anxious about my package. By the pump?"

"Yes, to your left as you go toward the front gate."

Prez trotted into the hall. Penner followed, held the front door open. The dog headed into the heavy falling snow. The grounds were two feet thick with new snow and Prez sank in and left dark holes as he went.

Penner slammed the front door, locked it. He ran through the rest of the house, locked doors, activated all the electric window locks and burglar bolts.

In the dining room he ordered a curry dinner.

The first thing Prez did was scratch at the front door, then the back. He barked, howled, shouted insults. Gale winds rose a little after ten and the sounds of the angry dog were muffled and lost.

By the time Penner went to bed the snow was coming in blizzard strength. There was no sound at all from Prez.

The breakfast-table radio said, "Present reports indicate all aboard the Swiss-bound New World Airlines autosonic superjet were lost when it went down in the storm-tossed Atlantic. Among those listed as passengers on the NWA flight are Asmund Crowden, the well-known investment broker, singer Merlo Benninger and Benny Maitland-Scott, lovely country-hopping daughter of the woolens tycoon. . . ."

Penner put down his coffee cup. He swooped an arm across the table and twisted up the volume.

The radio said, "Also said to be on the flight was former light-heavyweight champ, Kid. . . ."

There was a crackling and the sound died.

Penner hit the speaker grid with the heel of his hand. The little radio snapped, dislodged from its position on the table and fell. Penner ran to the living room and got the entertainment system warmed up. He flicked a toggle in the wall panel and the wall-size TV screen came alive.

"This is a cockatoo, of course, boys and girls," explained the plump man in the scarlet band uniform and curly red wig. "Isn't he handsome, Mr. Cracker-jacker?"

"I'll say, Cap. Oops, he nipped a little chunk out of your thumb."

"Son of a bitch," said the captain.

Penner hit at another switch. The Secretary of Defense appeared.

"I think we can level with each other, gentlemen. I have great respect for your committee and I say to you now in all honesty that we wouldn't drop anything like that on civilians."

On the next station a black man in a smock said, "Hello, Rick Martin here with the weather picture. As you can see by the map our computer is drawing for us, we Connecticut residents are in for more of the same. That's right, snow and more snow. Looks like the worst blizzard since the big one in nineteen-seventy-one."

Behind Penner a voice asked, "What's the excitement?"

"Prez—"

The floppy black dog was lolling in a flowered loveseat.

"No hard feelings," said the dog, scratching at his ear with his hind foot. "I guess you simply didn't realize I got locked out last night. You sure couldn't have heard my howling with the storm raging."

"How'd you get in?"

"I know a few tricks. Electronics tricks, simple

lock-picking," the dog told him. "You look unsettled."

Penner said, "The news. The news just said Benny's robot jet crashed."

Prez made an anguished whining sound.

"Benny? No. Are you sure she was on the plane?"

"Yes—they gave her name."

"There could be a mistake."

"You're right, Prez. I'll call the damn airline." He strode to the phone on the round marble coffee table. He picked up the reciever. "Damn it."

"What?"

"Line's dead."

"Happens during these blizzards. This isn't Manhattan or even the suburbs. Everything isn't underground yet in this neck of the woods. Trees fall over and disrupt the phone service."

Penner was in the hall. That phone was dead, too. He went through the big house and checked all the phones. He returned to the hall and snatched open the closet. He had his hand on a plaid neck scarf when Benny called to him.

"Norby. Norby, darling, where are you?"

Walking backward three steps, his fingers trailing the woolen scarf, Penner said carefully, "Benny?"

"Can you hear me? Oh, Norby, can you hear me across such a distance?"

She seemed to be in the living room. Penner stepped there.

"Benny, where are you?"

"I'm not sure, Norby. This is all very strange, isn't it? What a pleasant surprise, though, to discover that Defrocked Bishop Dix is right."

Her voice was coming from the dog.

Penner's arms involuntarily rose and his hands flapped faintly. He dropped the scarf, began breathing through his mouth.

"Benny, how in the hell did you get inside that damn dog?"

Prez's eyes were tightly closed and his mouth was barely open.

"I'm in the—well—what Defrocked Bishop Dix calls the Other Reality, Norby."

"Didn't you go to Switzerland?"

"Oh, Norby, darling, you are slow on the uptake, aren't you? Norby, I'm dead."

"Dead? No—"

"Yes. I'm here in the Other Reality now. But I can still talk to you sometimes. That'll be nice, won't it?"

Penner blinked, shook his head, gingerly picked up the dog.

"Benny, what are you saying?"

"I'm communicating with you from over here, Norby, through the spirit media. Don't ask me how or why, darling, but the best medium for communicating with you seems to be poor old Prez's electronic parts."

"Yes, but—" said Penner.

"Please stay there so I can talk to you, Norby. It's so strange here and I don't know anybody yet. Except for some of the people from the plane. You stay at the house until Dad can do something. And, Norby, I guess it's safe to tell you now I've mentioned you in my will."

Penner was face to face with the old dog.

"What's a girl twenty-two need a will for?"

"It came in handy, didn't it? Now that I'm deceased and all. I just want you to know you'll be provided for. You and poor dear Prez."

"I don't want to talk about that now, Benny."

"A half-million is all I could manage on my own for you, Norby. Is that going to be okay?"

Penner dropped the dog.

"A half a million dollars?"

Prez said, "Ouch. What's the idea, peckerwood?"

"Benny," called Penner.

"Are you getting unsettled some more?" Prez asked.

"Benny was just now talking to me. Through you, Prez. Didn't you hear it?"

"No." The dog jumped back up on the loveseat and arranged himself. "That's sort of marvelous in a way. Bishop Hix turns out to've been right, huh?"

"Bishop Dix. Defrocked Bishop Dix. He left the church."

"I guess you'd have to with all those wacky ideas."

"But it works, Prez. Benny can talk to me from— wherever she is."

The shaggy black dog scratched its ear.

"I think I'll go out and sniff around in the woods."

Penner said, "No. You stay right here."

"I have to go to the john," the dog said.

"I'll fix you up something in the rumpus room. You have to stay indoors. I don't want to risk you out in a blizzard. Benny will keep trying to get through. "

"Okay, I'll cooperate." The dog sniffed. "I'm hungry. Do you recall the lean red meat I alluded to last evening?"

"Sure, I'll get you a nice little steak and put it out in your dish."

"A big steak, peckerwood. And right here is where I'll eat it."

Penner said after a moment, "Okay, Prez."

Looking away from the electric typewriter, Penner watched the swirling snow outside the conservatory windows. The snow was four feet high and the wind roared and whooped. "I thought you had a special dictating machine for your correspondence," he said to Prez.

Prez was on a white leather sofa chair, worrying a steak bone.

He paused to say, "I'm not in the mood for that. It's more fun to dictate to you. Benny would help me out once in a while, too. Great fun on stormy days. Now get typing."

"A lot of fun—being private secretary to a mongrel dog," said Penner.

"What's that, peckerwood?"

"Nothing." Penner had talked to Benny twice more since that first time yesterday. He'd decided it was worth putting up with Prez if he could keep in contact with the girl. "Go ahead."

"Where was I?"

"'The sidemen on that particular session, my dear Derik, were Dicky Wells, Benny Carter, Wayman Carver, Leon "Chu" Berry. . . .' How may of these guys do you write to, Prez?"

"More than a hundred." The dog repositioned the bone with both front paws. "I'm in touch with more than a hundred jazz-buffs throughout the world. We exchange letters, records, tapes and other, sometimes exotic, memorabilia."

"Exotic?"

"The postal system is often very lax. We swap a few pills, a pinch of snuff now and then."

"You're a junkie?"

"No, I simply have a certain kind of scientific curiosity," replied the dog. "Let's get back to the letter at hand."

When Penner had typed three more letters and put them in envelopes he said, "Enough for today."

"Mail them now."

"There's not likely to be a pickup today."

"The post office will be open."

"It's two miles away and we're still having a blizzard."

He dropped the three letters down on the closed typewriter.

"I'm expecting a couple of more packages, too," the dog said.

"I'll go after the thaw."

"Today."

"Don't get arrogant, Prez."

"I'll go then."

The dog, bone in mouth, jumped to the floor.

"No you don't."

"Then, you."

Penner slowly inhaled and exhaled.

"I'll give it a try. You stay inside and if Benny tries to contact me, explain."

"Get a book of twelve-cent stamps while you're there."

Prez trotted out of the room.

Penner threw himself at the front door of the house, stumbled through it. He fell over the hall rug, crashed against the mail table on his way down, dropping two letters, a magazine and three packages. His face was frosted and a tingling red color. He did a lopsided pushup and worked to a sitting position. He unwound the cold and soggy woolen muffler with his stiff wool-mittened fingers.

"Norby, darling? Oh, my dearest, where are you?" called Benny's voice.

"In a minute, in a minute," he yelled back. "Hold on."

He grunted, tugged at his boots. These were slushy and dripped brown snow up his sleeves. He next rolled out of his snow coat.

"Norby, are you all right? Please talk to me. It's growing harder to reach you from over here. Such an effort is required."

"I'm coming, I'm coming. I've got problems, too, Benny."

He shed the rest of his outdoor clothes and went weaving into the living room.

Prez was on the floor near the magazine bin, on his back, feet up in the air.

"Norby, is something wrong?"

"I'm okay." Penner, squatting next to the dog, added: "Sometimes I wish you had worked out a better means of communication."

"I don't have much choice. Listen, Norby, it would be a great help if you could—"

"Could what?"

Prez opened his eyes.

"Where's the mail?"

Penner pinned the dog down by his shoulders.

"Benny, what is it you want?"

"Let go of me," said the dog.

Penner did.

The warm hand sat on his naked chest like a starfish. Penner sat up in the wide bed and said, "Yow."

"Norby, relax. You're certainly jumpy, aren't you?"

Penner reeled in the lamp cord and found the toggle. Light came on and he saw Benny, in a tan raincoat and dark head scarf, sitting on the edge of the bed.

He caught her elbow. The cloth was chill, still damp with the snowflakes.

"How does Bishop Dix work this?"

"What? I didn't mean to scare you awake, Norby. I know you weren't expecting me for several days. After the flight was canceled I spent the night in New York. I called you first thing the next morning but the phone was out. So I decided to fight my way back to you and here—finally—I am."

She leaned down to kiss him.

"Then you didn't go down in the storm-tossed waters of the Atlantic?"

"Our flight was canceled," said the lovely blond girl. "I phoned Dad and he said he'd make other arrangements. So I rented a car and I got stuck in Port Chester for the longest spell—but here I am."

Penner touched her again.

"Benny, about Prez?"

"Is he well? The cold bothers him sometimes."

"He's fine. Can he change his voice at all? That is, have you ever known him to do something like that?"

Benny laughed.

"Has he been teasing you? Yes, he's very good at impersonations. We had that built in."

Penner said, "You stay here. I'll be back in a few minutes. A last-minute something I thought of."

"Can't it wait?"

"No."

"I'll take off my clothes."

"Do that," he said.

Penner grabbed a robe and shuffled into slippers. He
shot out of the bedroom and down the stairs. Prez was
gone from the loveseat he had selected to sleep on.
Penner chose the heaviest poker from the rack of them
screwed to the fireplace bricks. He roamed the dark
house and located the shaggy black dog under an old
desk in the rumpus room.

"Come out of there, you bastard."

The dog huddled in a nest of torn package wrappings.
A Swedish stamp had gotten stuck to his floppy left ear.

"What is it now, peckerwood?"

Penner said, "We've sure had a lot of fun. You and
your damn hoax. Well, as you must know, Benny's
back. I'm going to run things."

"That'll be a switch."

Penner thrust his free hand under the desk and caught
at Prez.

"Watch it—"

Prez snarled, then bit Penner's hand.

"Damn." Penner pulled his bleeding hand free. "Now
you're really through, Prez."

"Oh, no" said the dog. "You are."

"What?"

"You've just been infected with rabies."

Penner looked from his injured hand to the dog under
the desk.

"No more jokes, Prez. I happen to know there hasn't
been a case of rabies in this part of the country for ten
years."

"I know," said the dog. "That's why I had to send
away for the virus."

✿ Confessions

The stubby man pounded his fist on the patio table. He then looked hopefully across at Jose Silvera. "That's about how I've been doing it."

"Basically," said the tall, wide-shouldered Silvera, "Your table-pounding is okay."

Hugo Kohinoor brought his still-fisted hand up and rubbed his outspread stomach. "Not a great table thump, though, is it, Joe?"

Silvera studied the clear blue afternoon sky. He stroked his chin with the chill rim of his ale mug. "When

I suggested you had a problem, I meant not with how you pound the table but when. The point being that the fault isn't really in those speeches I wrote for you."

A waiter in a white flannel surcoat came trotting over. "You don't have to hammer on your table, I was coming."

"We don't really want you," Kohinoor told him. "I was only practicing."

The waiter bent and scrutinized the pudgy man. "Ah," he said. "You're Hugo Kohinoor, head of the Cultural Surveillance Agency for our entire planet of Murdstone." From a flap pocket of his surcoat he took a pair of lemon-yellow spectacles and clamped them on. "You don't look as squabbish in person as you do on the lecture platform."

"Thank you," said the CSA head.

"Another ale," mentioned Silvera. Rose-tinted gulls were spiraling down through the sky to skim the calm waters of the bay.

"I must tell you, Mr. Kohinoor," contiued the waiter, "I was deeply moved by your recent speech at our Melazo Territory Citizens Club. Usually I don't pay much attention to a squatty man. You, however, have something to say and you say it well."

"How about when I pounded my fist on the lectern? Was that attention-getting?"

"It was the day I heard you," replied the waiter, "because you knocked over the water carafe." He bowed. "I'll fetch your order now. One ale? Good. Keep up your fine work, Mr. Kohinoor."

Kohinoor smiled at Silvera. "He seemed sincere in his appreciation."

"The speeches are fine," said Silvera. "So pay me the rest of the money."

Kohinoor said, "At first I thought $1500 for only three speeches attacking the . . . what was it you called them?"

"Lords of the press. You still owe me $750."

"Freedom of the press is a flaming sword. That's how it goes, right? Freedom of the press is a flaming sword and I am here to tell you that the lords of the press have turned that sword into a lawnmower which is nipping in the bud the free flow of thought. Yes, that's nicely put."

Silvera nodded and picked up the fresh ale the waiter had brought. "When you recited it just now you hit the table on *here* and *lawnmower.*"

"Not effective?"

Silvera said, "On *flaming sword* you ought to wave your hand in the air. Then after *free flow* you let it fall with a thud and smash into the table. You'll get applause."

"They have been applauding on lawnmower and I was wondering why," admitted Kohinoor. "Traveling around the planet a lot you sometimes get confused. Melazo Territory is mostly resort country and there's nothing like a lawnmower industry here. Now I understand."

"Cash if you have it."

Kohinoor reached into his knickers and pulled out his wallet. "I'm sorry I criticized the speeches, Joe. Actually, you did a fine job. Is one 50 and seven 100s okay?"

"Yes." Silvera took the cash, folded his hand over it. He was reaching for his own wallet when a three-story 'wooden house flew over. He jumped up and ran to the marble rail of the resort hotel patio. The black house was flying over at about two thousand feet. Silvera shook his head and returned to the statesman's table. "Those bastards," he said, sitting again.

"Who? The Blackhawk Group?"

"Yes. You know them?"

"I'm a close friend of Professor Burton Prester-Johns," said Kohinoor. "McLew Scribbeley, who, as I understand, is the legal owner of Blackhawk Manor, I've had a few conflicts with. Because of that Scribbeley Press of his. Basically, though, I'm fond of all the writers in the Blackhawk Group."

Silvera said, "McLew Scribbeley owes me $2000."

"I thought it was part of your code as a free-lance writer, Joe, to always collect your fees."

"I do," said Silvera, "usually. These Blackhawk people keep moving their house."

"A delightful novelty, I think. Flying mobile homes. I'd like to settle down like that someday."

"I've tracked McLew Scribbeley to three different territories on Murdstone so far," said Silvera.

"Did you write something for that vile Scribbeley Press of his?"

"Yes, three confessions," said Silvera. "I did *Confessions of a Robust Man*, *My Disgusting Sex Life* and *I, a Rascal*."

Kohinoor blinked his little blue eyes. "You mean you're A Man of High Station, Dr. X and Anonymous? I had them down in my Cultural Surveillance files as three separate authors."

"I can write in different styles."

"That one, that *My Disgusting Sex Life*," said Kohinoor. "I found it to be . . . disgusting."

Silvera asked, "Do you know where he's going to land that damn house this time?"

"Yes, on Post Road Hill," said Kohinoor. "As a matter of fact, I'm invited there to dinner tonight."

Silvera frowned. "I'll come along."

Two hundred bicycles came clattering down over the crest of the hill, each ridden by a shouting adolescent. Silvera caught the squat Kohinoor by the fur collar of his formal doublet and hauled him back against their just-landed cruiser. Even so, a passing handlebar whacked the surveillance chief in the elbow.

"Long live Prester-Johns!" cried the cycling youths as they rattled by Blackhawk Manor and on downhill.

Kohinoor said, "Cyclemania has caught up the youth of Murdstone."

"Yes, I saw your friend Prester-Johns talking about it on television last night."

"Old P-J relates to youth in ways some of us can't, and he's nearly sixty," said Kohinoor. "Of course, he's a tall man. It's easier to radiate charisma when you've got height."

After the last cyclist had passed Silvera and Kohinoor crossed the wide dirt roadway and walked to the iron gate that stood at the edge of the wooded acres the Blackhawk mansion now occupied. A frail man in an ironmonger's tunic peered up over a hedge. "Don't use the gate yet, gentleman."

"Why?"

"It's not screwed to the fence," explained the workman. "I only now got the thing uncrated. See, one of the delays was the box with the razor-sharp fence spikes got misplaced. What is more, the nitwit movers threw out the ground glass I'm supposed to sprinkle atop the stone wall out back. See, they opened the box and saw all that broken glass and felt responsible. So they ditched the glass, box and all. Well, come around through here."

"Thank you," said the stubby Kohinoor.

Silvera helped him get over the hedges and onto the path.

"Oh, sirs," called the ironmonger as they started up the winding gravel pathway to the house. "You're the final guests of the evening. So you can tell them to turn on the watchdogs in another fifteen minutes. I'll be finished by then."

"Scribbeley and P-J have a dozen robot hounds," said Kohinoor.

"I've encountered them," said Silvera.

"Did you notice that some of those young girls on the bicycles weren't wearing much, Joe?"

"A few of them were naked."

"Should I be for or against that I wonder," reflected the stumpy man. "The kids are holding their big annual bike-in some three miles from here all this week. Perhaps I should issue a position paper. You could write one up for me. Do you know anything about naked bicycle riding?"

"I've done it." They climbed up the red stone steps of the dark wood mansion.

"Oh, really? I guess when you freelance you have more spare time for fooling around." Kohinoor used the golden hawkshead knocker on the door.

The butler was pale, dressed in shades of gray. "Good evening, Mr. Kohinoor." He glanced then at Silvera. "Yipes." He backed and ran off along the flowered hall carpeting.

"I've encountered him before, too." Silvera walked into the house.

In a huge oak-paneled room at the hall's end were gathered several people. The butler had not gone there, but up a curving staircase to the second floor. In the paneled room a piano stopped playing and then a muscular man in a tweed oversuit leaped out into the hall. He had an upthrust jaw, square teeth and shaggy blond hair. "Well, well, Kohinoor, you old bastard. Was it you spooked Dwiggins?"

"No, Henry." He pointed a thumb at Silvera. "This is my friend, Jose Silvera. The sight of him seemed to startle poor Dwiggins."

"Silvera, Silvera," said the tweedy man. "You write, too, don't you?"

"That's right, Dobbs."

Henry Verner Dobbs nodded, his chin bobbed. "Know me, know me, do you? Or more likely my work. I'm Henry Verner Dobbs, the author. My specialty is deluxe war books. You probably encountered my photo on the back of my latest hit, *The Coffee Table Book of Hand Grenades*. Big mother of a book, weighs eleven pounds. We, my publishers and I, had it printed on the planet Tarragon by zombies. Those little zombie bastards do lovely color plates, and cheap."

Silvera circled around Dobbs and went into the living room. Scribbeley, the publisher who owed him $2000, wasn't there. Seated at the grand piano was a lovely girl of twenty-six, a tall coltish brunette with deeply tanned skin and a slight feverish flush.

"Why, it's Jose Silvera," said this lovely girl now. Her voice had a gentle throaty sound. "I've been an admirer of yours since I was a convent girl."

"You've read the fellow's work?" asked the thin white-haired man standing near the piano.

"I've never read his books, no," said the girl. "I never read other writers. But I saw a picture of Mr. Silvera on a book jacket and I swiped the book. Clipped the photo and kept it pasted inside the cover of my breviary. A good many authors are so unauspicious-looking. Mr.

Silvera is, on the other hand, big and cute. I am Willa de Aragon, Mr. Silvera." She left the tufted piano bench and came over to him. She touched his hand with her very warm fingers, smiling.

"Do you have a fever?" asked Silvera.

"No, I'm naturally very intense and it seems to heat my body up," she answered. "What brings you to Blackhawk Manor, Mr. Silvera? My invitation didn't mention you."

"Aren't you the fellow?" asked the thin old man.

Kohinoor came hurrying over. "This is Jose Silvera, P-J. Joe, this is Burton Prester-Johns, one of our leading philosophers."

"Aren't you the fellow who threw Dwiggins out of the greenhouse?"

"Into," said Silvera.

"Whichever direction, it played havoc with the glass panels. We had to abandon the greenhouse, in fact. It's grounded, won't fly. Yes, you're that fellow."

"Joe is a very talented and affable person." Kohinoor reached over and pounded on the piano top. "I brought him along tonight, P-J, so he and McLew Scribbeley can settle their differences for good and all."

"Kind of fellow who throws butlers through greenhouse walls," said Prester-Johns. "Not the kind of fellow one can trust. Yes, it's no small wonder our young people have more faith in bicycles than in their elders." He rubbed a sharp forefinger in the opposite palm. "As I summed up the situation in *Bikocracy*, the responsibility for. . . ."

"Shall I give, shall I give him the heave-ho?" Dobbs had leaped back into the room.

"Well, he isn't the kind of fellow one wants to get cozy with."

Kohinoor hit the piano again. "You have to be less

suspicious, P-J. Just because the Commando Killer is still loose, you don't have to be so cautious."

Prester-Johns inhaled so deeply he tipped over slightly. He touched his lined cheek with one thin hand.

Dobbs said, "Uh."

Her breath warm, Willa whispered to Silvera, "They have a rule never to talk about the Commando Killer within these walls."

"Why?"

"Apparently, Mr. Silvera, this fiend who has been roaming Murdstone for nearly a year now, claiming a score of victims," said the warm girl. "Apparently this fiend has struck several times in the vicinity of Blackhawk Manor. If you are aware how mobile Blackhawk is you'll know this involves several separate vicinities."

Through the arched entranceway came a fat man in a white suit. He had a bristling red mustache and a ribbed bald head. "Throw out that wop," he said, pointing at Silvera. "Hello, wop." He chuckled. "Only kidding, Joe. Who cares if you're a dago?" He came closer to Silvera. "The throw you out on your keaster part is true. Dwiggins just went to get a couple of my hunkie retainers. Just kidding. I don't hold their race against them." He shot out his hand suddenly and pinched Willa's left buttock. "Hi, there, you sex-crazed little wench. Just kidding, Willa."

Silvera noticed Scribbeley's suit was one that had the currently fashionable lapels. He grabbed these and wrenched the publisher up off the floor. "Two thousand dollars."

"Jose, what did I tell your agent, that sweet little Jenny Jennings?"

"Nothing. You pinched her ankle and that was it."

"I was aiming for her left buttock," said the fat publisher. "Look, Joe, I confess I have a compulsive desire to pinch girls. I swear to you that is my only fault. I told your agent and now I tell you, I never got paid by my distributor. Take that one title you did. *My Disgusting Sex Life*. We got a lot of negative mail from people saying it wasn't disgusting. Incidents like that can make people lose faith in Scribbeley Press."

"Two thousand dollars," repeated Silvera, dropping Scribbeley.

"I could let you have eighty-six thousand unbound copies of *I, a Rascal*, Joe. You could maybe bind them in a nice sensual cloth and make a fortune selling them mail-order."

"Cash, now," said Silvera. Then something came down and hit his head. It hit him hard and several times and he fell down.

Silvera awoke in midair. He hit on his side in among piles of fresh-cut shrub, some hundred yards from Blackhawk Manor. He saw, by squinting through the branches and leaves his head was lodged among, three of Scribbeley's henchmen strutting back toward the turreted mansion.

Extracting his left arm from thorned branches, Silvera knifed his hand in alongside his stuck head and got the thorns away from his cheek. He gave a grunt and pulled back and out free. He stood up and a black dog bounded over and bit him in the leg. Its teeth were stainless steel and penetrated quite deep. Silvera took a small tool kit out of an inside pocket and, recalling a diagram he'd consulted at the Melazo Territory Free Library that afternoon, he deactivated and then dismantled the mechanical dog.

He dropped the dog components in with the shrub and brush that had been cleared away to make landing room for the mansion. Silvera nodded, looked at the newly arrived moon, stepped into the pine woods that surrounded the mansion site. He worked his way quietly back toward the house, favoring his injured leg.

Silvera worked slowly through the woods and emerged at the rear of the mansion. Through the lighted windows of the kitchen he saw a robot pastry chef filling creampuffs. Crouched low, Silvera approached the twenty wooden steps leading up to the pantry door.

Three more mechanical dogs came around a black edge of the house. They didn't bark, giving out instead a beeping siren sound. One of them had eyes that flashed a bile yellow.

Silvera ran. They pursued him twice around a sundial and once through the still empty fishpond.

"Do come in, Mr. Silvera," called a sweet voice from a quickly opened door below the pantry stairs.

He obliged. Silvera ducked through the storeroom doorway and Willa de Aragon slammed the thick door against the vinyl muzzle of the yellow-eyed hound. "Thanks," said Silvera.

The slim glowing girl held her hand torch toward his injured leg. "You've sustained a wound, Mr. Silvera. You're lucky they haven't had time to unpack the rabies and other poisons for the fangs."

"You were coming out to look for me?"

"I was concerned and I thought I might be able to help out. I believe your friend, Mr. Kohinoor, was talking about going to bring you back but he hasn't as yet." She touched one warm hand to his cheek. "Whenever I'm a house guest at Blackhawk Manor I insist on a room with a secret passage." She gracefully crossed the musty room and pointed at a slid-open portion of the raw wood wall. "By going up a little narrow stairway you're in my bedchamber. There's an adjoining bath and I'll be able to minister to your wounds."

"Okay," said Silvera. The girl smiled and stepped into the dark hole. He followed, asking, "Won't they miss you?"

"I can join them for dinner later perhaps," said the warm girl.

Her bedroom was large, with flocked rosebuds on the walls and a pastoral scene painted on the slightly domed ceiling. There were thick rugs, thick tapestries, thick draperies and a huge hand-carved bed. A six-prong candelabra stood on a round marble table near the bed.

As Silvera stepped out of the wall he heard an odd clattering down on the grounds. He pulled aside a wine-colored drape at the nearest window and looked out. A tall young man was walking a bicycle into the pine woods. A moment later, without the cycle, he came walking by the sundial and then was out of sight. The dogs didn't bother him.

"Would you mind taking off your pants?" asked Willa. "Before I turned to authorship I worked as a practical nurse in a satellite gambling hall orbiting Tarragon. I can treat your injuries quite professionally you'll find, Mr. Silvera."

He left the window and moved toward the pale blue bathroom the lovely girl was stepping into. He stopped at the threshold, unseamed his trousers and, after getting out of his boots, dropped the trousers. "What sort of writing do you do, Willa?"

She nudged a knee-high white wicker hamper toward him. "Sit on that," she said. "Well, Mr. Silvera, there is a genre of novels which is quite popular here on Murdstone at the moment. They're known as Gothics, though I'm not sure why. All about sensitive young girls who are put upon by strange dark men in sinister old houses in out of the way places."

"Yes, I wrote a dozen of them when there was a Gothic craze on Barnum five years ago," he said, sitting. The mechanical dog bite didn't look too bad.

"Under your own name?" She cleansed the wound.

"No, I was," said Silvera, remembering, "Anna Mary Windmiller."

Willa stopped applying a bandage. "My goodness, Mr. Silvera. You don't mean to tell me you are Anna Mary Windmiller?"

"A dozen times I was anyway," he said. "They were paying $1500 per book."

"You've been an inspiration to me, those books have been. Why, I carry tattered, much-read copies with me still," said Willa. "I am particularly fond of *The Crumbling Château on Grave Spawn Hill*. Though *Return to the Crumbling Château on Grave Spawn Hill* is nearly as moving. The opening lines of the former I think are excellent and exemplary: 'I confess a sense of dark chagrin flowed through my young, recently graduated from a quiet girls school, frame when I first opened the door of that crumbling house and tripped over the lifeless body of the local vicar.' A brilliant piece of writing, I think. Oh, I only wish I could write my own Gothics half as well." She finished the bandage and stepped up and back. "Are you violently anxious to rush right down and collect your money?"

"Not violently. Eventually I'm going to get the $2000 from Scribbeley, though. Why?"

"It seems a shame, since you already have your

trousers off, not to go to bed together, don't you think?"

Silvera rose from the wicker hamper. "You're pretty aggressive for a writer of polite ladies' fiction."

"Yes," admitted Willa, "and I fear it shows in my work at times."

Silvera smiled, picked her up off the blue tiles and carried her into the bedroom.

It wasn't until the next morning that Silvera left Willa. When he tried to get downstairs by way of the hall, he was stopped by a uniformed police captain.

The policeman, who'd appeared around a turn in the broad curved stairway, said, "You might as well come join the suspects, sir. Do you happen to know where Miss de Aragon is at the moment?"

"Putting on her shoes," said Silvera. "Suspects for what?"

"The murder, sir," said the man in the seagreen uniform. "The inspector is waiting in the living room. Don't try to escape, by the way, as there are vicious dogs outside."

"I know about the dogs."

"Not those robot mutts. We brought our own."

Silvera shrugged his broad shoulders slightly and descended. As he stepped into the living room McLew Scribbeley called out, "Hello, killer."

Silvera stopped beside a marble statue of a fawn.

"The man who jumps to conclusions often lands on unfirm ground," said a roundheaded man in a plaid greatcoat.

"Just kidding," said Scribbeley.

"I am Inspector Ludd," said the roundheaded man. "I would like to know who you are."

"He's the fellow who brought the victim," put in Prester-Johns, who was dressed in a paisley lounging robe this morning.

"I'm Jose Silvera. Kohinoor's been killed?"

"Death is like a loose shingle," said the inspector, "that falls on whoever is passing beneath. Yes, Hugo Kohinoor is dead, the victim, so it appears, of the Commando Killer." He had a sliding walk and he made a sort of skating motion approaching Silvera. "Sometimes memory is like a garbage truck with some valuable object thrown away by mistake and lost among coffee grounds and watermelon rinds. Forgive me for not recognizing you sooner, Silvera."

"Since we've never met, it's okay."

"You are the same Jose Silvera who has done such excellent articles for the *Interplanetary Real Crime* magazine?"

"I did a series on pattern killers for them once, yes."

"Modesty here is of no more use than a bunch of bananas in a lion's den," said Inspector Ludd. "I'd appreciate your help on this investigation, Silvera."

Dobbs leaped in, eating the last of a square waffle. "He's probably the murderer. I doubt he'll be much help," said the war book author.

"Please accompany me to the site of the crime, Silvera," suggested the inspector. "I'll continue this series of interviews later."

"I have an autographing party at a bookshop this noon," said Dobbs. "They're going to unload a hundred remaindered copies of my *Picture History of Poison Gas*."

"Murder, though he often arrives late, takes the best seat in the house," said Inspector Ludd with a half-round smile.

"What does that mean?"

"It means, Mr. Dobbs, no one can leave Blackhawk Manor until this investigation has been concluded," said the inspector. To Scribbeley he added, "It means, too, the scene of the crime cannot leave either. Don't go flying off in this mobile home of yours."

"We're renting this location for a month," said Prester-Johns. "I'm to lecture at the Bike-in all this week and then I'll be doing a little tramp cycling act for the young people on the weekend."

"Perhaps," said the Inspector. He led Silvera outside.

Standing on the fresh earth at the edge of the woods, Inspector Ludd said, "You can see why this murderer has earned the name of Commando Killer, Silvera. Notice the use of the bayonet, plus the garrote. There are several other little military touches as well. You were here all night, Silvera?"

"Yes. When was Kohinoor killed?"

"Probably between 3 *A.M.* and dawn," said Ludd. "Did you notice anything unusual?"

"I must have slept through the murder." Silvera knelt down beside the body of Kohinoor. "Little scrap of paper between his thumb and forefinger."

"Yes, it is the corner of a $100 Murdstone currency bill. We are hopeful of finding the rest of it."

"What do they say in the house?" Silvera got to his feet.

"Kohinoor stayed to dinner, though angry because you'd been roughly handled," said the roundheaded inspector. "Most everyone retired at midnight or thereabouts. No one admits to being out here at all. Kohinoor was not supposed to have stayed overnight. One of the men coming to finish setting up the new greenhouse found his body here shortly before breakfast. You spent the night with Miss de Aragon?"

"Yes."

"I deduced as much from her reported absence at dinner last evening and from what I've heard of you," said Inspector Ludd. "Added to the fact you are still here many hours after you were ejected. I don't think, though, you would have killed Kohinoor over a fee."

"I never do that, no," said Silvera. "I either collect my money or I don't. Most often I do."

"That free-lance life," said the inspector with a sigh. "I chose the security of a civil job rather than attempt it. You may have noted my speech is frequently spiced with aphorisms."

"Yes, I noticed."

"The remnants of an ambition to be a lyric poet," said Inspector Ludd. "Did you know that when the Commando Killer struck two months ago in Esfola Territory he was seen and they got a description plus composite sketches?"

"No, it hasn't been in the news."

"Not as yet," said the inspector. "In a way it is disappointing. This Blackhawk house has been in the vicinity of almost all the attacks by the Commando Killer and neither I nor any of the other investigators across Murdstone can link anyone in Blackhawk Manor with these crimes."

"Fingerprints, footprints?"

"No fingerprints and the only footprint we've found this time is that one there. We've made a cast of it."

"Belongs to nobody at the house?"

"It was made by an old commando boot of extremely large size. We haven't as yet located one inside, though my men are still searching," said the inspector. "The description and the eyewitness sketches I've gone over of the brute looks like no one here."

"A disguise maybe."

"No," said Ludd. "Look at that footprint. The fellow is a giant and a brutal-looking shaggy fellow." He sighed again. "We rounded up all the giant brutal shaggy fellows in our files and got nothing. So I think. . . ."

"What?"

"You no doubt recall the famous Nolan and Anmar case on Venus a generation ago."

"Double personality. Nolan turned himself into Anmar with a pill he'd invented."

"Exactly," said Ludd. "I have the feeling something similar may be involved here. Though there is no proof of any such thing."

Silvera scratched at the back of his neck. "The kid on the bicycle," he said.

"We found cycle tracks in the woods, yes. But no bike and no cyclist on the premises. No one admits having had such a visitor either. What do you know?"

"Something about that kid," said Silvera. "I saw him get here about nine last night, park his bicycle in the woods and sneak into Blackhawk Manor through the back way. Yes, and he was one of the kids who came by earlier on the way to the Bike-in."

"You could recognize him?"

"Sure."

"We'll go looking at the Bike-in," the inspector said. "Sometimes the slenderest thread unravels the most of the sweater." He smiled at Silvera. "A sample of my aphoristic style."

Silvera smiled briefly.

Silvera walked among hundreds of parked cycles and around groups singing bicycle songs and groups taking off each other's clothes and groups dismantling and rebuilding bikes. All on a rolling grassy plain with a wide roadway bordering part of it.

"You look awfully old to be a bike person," said a half-dressed girl who was leaning against a unicycle.

"I thought so, too," answered Silvera, "until I fell under the spell of Burton Prester-Johns."

"That old twit," said the girl, rubbing her bare freckled stomach. "He's disgusting. Whenever I see someone over thirty riding a bicycle it makes me retch and gag."

"Those are interesting symptoms." Silvera glanced away from the girl and spotted Inspector Ludd wandering down through the crowds from the opposite side of the plain. "I'm looking for a guy who rides a 10-speed black Martian Wollter brand bike. Lean guy, sandy hair, little mustache."

"Are you a law person? Law people make me have severe pains in the lower abdomen."

"I'm a free-lance journalist researching an in-depth story on the bicycle culture."

"That's repellent," said the girl. "Old gents way up in their thirties trying to understand youth. That makes me writhe and have severe chills."

"Maybe you ought to be home in bed."

"That's all you old boys think of."

Silvera walked on. Then over in the afternoon shade of a refreshment stand he saw the sandy-haired boy. He caught the inspector's eye and nodded toward the stand.

The two of them began working through the crowd and toward the boy, who had one elbow against the yellow wall of the stand and was drinking a mug of May Wine.

The boy sensed Silvera while he was still two hundred

feet from him. He recognized Silvera apparently, turned on his left toes and ran off.

Silvera began to run, too, shouldering through cyclists. A plump albino boy took offense and threw his May wine in Silvera's face. Silvera kept running, wiping strawberries off his coat. He dashed around the refreshment stand, saw the boy starting up the plain toward the roadway, riding now on his black 10-speed bike.

Silvera stopped and grabbed up a parked 3-speed local bike. He only covered twenty feet before a girl cried out, "Aged bicycle thief!"

Three cycle singers leaped up, swinging lutes and mandolins.

Silvera pedaled hard. Four more boys came after him. They tackled both Silvera and the borrowed bike.

Leaving the bike seat, Silvera was carried ten feet and then dumped on the short grass. Before any of the four boys could jump on him he rolled, bowling over a picnic lunch for three. At the far side of the picnic drop cloth Silvera regained his feet. He ran, zigzagging, after the escaping boy.

He was tackled again, by three chunky girls in blue leather jerkins this time, a few yards short of the roadway. "Nasty old man," said one girl, hitting him up beside the ear with a bicycle pump.

"I'm only thirty-three," explained Silvera, ducking away from a second swing of the hard metal pump.

"Well, that's plenty old."

"Stop! The hand that takes up the sword against another often unsheaths more than it bargains for."

"What?" asked the girl who was jumping on Silvera's stomach with her bent knees.

Inspector Ludd, panting, said, "I mean he who would wear the judge's wig must first be abundantly certain he has the right-sized head."

"Drop the aphorisms," said Silvera, "and tell them you're a cop."

The three blocky girls stopped attacking Silvera. "You're a cop, granpappy?"

"Inspector Ludd of the Municipal Police, yes," said Ludd. "I have been trying to suggest that you ought to leave law enforcement to me."

As the girls drifted away Silvera got himself up off the grass. "That was the kid I saw last night. He seems to have gotten away from us."

"I know who he is," said Inspector Ludd. "Which puts us one step closer to the solution."

Silvera decided to sit down again for a moment. "The greatest journeys often begin with a single step," he said and began dusting himself off.

The day ended and rain began to fall with the darkness. A rough wind came blowing through the pine woods and rattled the spires and shutters and dark carved wood of Blackhawk Manor. In the living room a fire was starting to take hold in the deep tile-bordered fireplace.

Inspector Ludd had taken off his plaid greatcoat and was in his dark two-piece civilian suit, pacing.

Dobbs said, "How can we reenact the crime, Inspector?" He sipped at the glass of wine that had been passed to him a moment before by Dwiggins. "We are fairly certain, aren't we, this Commando Killer is someone from the outside, who more or less by coincidence, by repeated coincidence, happens to commit his crimes around our house. I'm no crime expert, like you and your boy Silvera. No, since my time is given over to the study of somewhat more important matters. Military matters. Such as the new book I'm putting together, *The Picture History of Trenches.*"

When everyone had been served a drink, the inspector said, "First, Silvera, tell them what we have found out."

Silvera was on the piano bench next to Willa. He lifted his hand from the small of her back and said, "A young guy named Roberto Koop came here on his bicycle last evening."

"Friend of yours, isn't he?" McLew Scribbeley asked his philosopher housemate.

"I'm not intimate with everyone who rides a bike," said Prester-Johns. "Possibly I met the young fellow during one of my encounters with our new bikocracy. What does he say?"

"The young man is being sought at the moment," said Inspector Ludd.

"The point is," said Silvera, "Koop has an uncle, Professor LeRoy Koop. Professor Koop has been doing some military research for the Murdstone Combined Armed Forces."

"Wait now," Dobbs interupted. "That CAF stuff is all very secret."

"Inspector Ludd has been allowed to sit in on some of the briefings," said Silvera. "So he knows young Koop's uncle has developed a new drug and it's known as Military Pills."

"These Military Pills," explained the inspector, "can turn any average recruit into a giant vicious fighting man."

"I've never heard of them," said Dobbs.

"The Military Pills have been developed and completely tested. They were ready for extended use over three years ago," continued the inspector. "That they have not been widely used as yet is due to the fact the

Combined Armed Forces have been tangled up in an ethical debate.''

"We contacted Professor Koop late this afternoon," said Silvera. He hadn't touched his wine as yet. Setting the glass on the piano, he stood. "Koop eventually admitted young Roberto Koop had swiped several hundred Military Pills from him over a year ago and gone into hiding. He's apparently learned how to make the stuff and has been selling Military Pills through the underside of the territories. Some of his customers are probably higher placed. One of them, someone who has found the pills to be addictive, is in the house here.''

Inspector Ludd said, "We were able to borrow some sample pills from Professor Koop." He smiled his half-round smile at them all. "A little earlier Silvera discovered an important clue. Because of his particular orientation he figured out where the Commando Killer had hidden his boots. We now have them.''

"Where does that get you?'' asked Prester-Johns.

"The Commando Killer," said Silvera, "is one of you. He takes the Military Pills and changes into a giant shaggy killer. All we have to do now is see who fits into the boots.''

"They won't fit anybody," said Willa. "If this killer is a dual personality. I mean, it's his alter feet you want.''

"Exactly," said the inspector. "Which is why we dissolved several of the tasteless Military Pills in your wine. Our discussion has gone on until everyone has finished his first glass. The drug, for those of you who aren't familiar with it, takes roughly fifteen minutes to take effect and lasts for two to three hours.''

All the lights went out.

Silvera, as he'd rehearsed earlier, ran across the room and through a side door. He sprinted down a dark hallway and through another doorway. In this new dark room he got behind a full-length drape and waited.

In less than a minute a panel in the wall slid open and McLew Scribbeley stepped into the room. He turned on a desk lamp and got down on his hands and knees in front of a globe of the planet mounted on a tripod. He spun the Murdstone globe three times to the left, three to the right, once to the left. Then he pressed his fingers on five separate cities. The large globe clicked open, one quarter of it swinging out. Scribbeley thrust a hand inside. He raked out packets of paper money first, bags of coin next. Then he yanked out a giant pair of muddy commando boots. "That's odd," he muttered. "They're still here."

"We were just kidding." Silvera was out from behind the drapes, a small hand blaster aimed at the kneeling publisher. "I'd figured it was you and we wanted to see where you had the damn shoes hidden. So we told you we'd already found them and you couldn't keep yourself from coming here to see if it was so."

"What do you know?" said Scribbeley. "How'd you decide it was me?"

"Most of the murders have been motiveless," said Silvera. "Something you couldn't help once the Military Pills got hold of you. You probably tried the stuff in the first place to boost your virility but it didn't work out that way. Last night, though, you had a real reason for the killing. Kohinoor, I figure, came to you and pressured you. He was angry about the way you'd handled my complaints. He probably threatened to crack down on your book enterprises if you didn't settle. So you told him you'd pay him the $2000 you owed me. You told him to meet you outside after everybody'd turned in. You gave him the cash and while he was still in the woods you turned into your killer side."

"Son of a gun," said Scribbeley, standing by pressing on his knees. "You sure are a smart one, you dago rascal. Well, I confess you're absolutely correct. The thing you've overlooked is that I'm going to change into the Commando Killer. When I do your little gun won't stop me." He paused, then roared and came at Silvera. He ran halfway to the window and then stopped, frowning at his hands. "That's odd, I'm not changing. Even though you put the stuff in the drinks."

"We were kidding about that, too," Silvera said.

Inspector Ludd came in from the hall with one of his captains. "A shot fired while blindfolded still sometimes finds a worthwhile target." They took Scribbeley from the room.

When Willa came to find Silvera a few moments later, he was at the globe. "Are you all right, Mr. Silvera?"

"Wait until I count out two thousand of this."

"All that cash and you're only taking two thousand?"

"That's all he owed me," said Silvera.

Monte Cristo Complex ⚙

Of all the cases impressed on my memory banks I think the affair of the man known as The Dismantler was one of the most interesting Vincent Hawthorn ever investigated. It got going on a warm, moderately smoggy day toward the end of 2031. Hawthorn was standing, rocking from foot to foot, by the view window of his tower suite and watching what could be seen of Greater Los Angeles. The view that day was limited to the smeared lower portions of the many rancho-style apartment towers that surround us.

Hawthorn was a tall husky man with close-cropped black hair and a fuzzy beard that made an O around his mouth. Throughout all of Greater Los Angeles, from the Santa Barbara Sector to the San Diego Sector, Hawthorn was known as one of the top men in the field of psychiatric crime detection.

"DBA-51," he said to me, turning from the vista, "why don't you chill a bottle of Pasadena '19?"

As you may know, after they let all those germs loose in Europe during the war scare of 1997, the wine industry there was pretty much finished. Southern California had since then moved into a prominent position in the production of wine. "I'd suggest rather a dry Azusa '21."

Hawthorn shook his head. "No, DBA-51." His tone implied that here was an area where even a high-grade android such as myself might go astray.

I shifted one shoulder. "Someone at the door," I said, rising. One of the things programmed into me is a slight sense of anticipation. As I neared the pale blue metal door the soft chimes sounded.

"Who do you think it is?" asked Hawthorn.

"Police." I opened the door and let in small spare Captain Korngold of the Police Service.

"We've got a beautiful one for you, Vincent," said the captain, after he and I had shaken hands.

Hawthorn fiddled with the seam of his smoking jacket, resealed it. "Round up a bottle of Glendale, DBA-51, and some glasses." He sat down in the black wing chair he liked to listen to police problems in.

"Over at Justice Hall," began Captain Korngold, "we refer to this fellow as The Dismantler."

"What fellow?"

"Day before yesterday he laid waste to an automatic

dance hall over on Main," said the captain. "Took the clockworks out of seven tap dancers and then dismantled a professor of the tango. It was all cogs and springs around the place."

"Not another Samson complex," muttered Hawthorn.

"Wait now," said Korngold as I handed him his glass of the pale dry Glendale wine. "Yesterday, about eleven in the morning, he struck again. We get descriptions of him but we can't seem to get our hands on him. We ran the descriptions through R&I and they fit 42,000 men so far. Five feet ten, age about thirty-five. Brown hair, no scars. Wearing a light brown one zipper suit, carrying a tool kit."

My own memory banks contain all the data the Police Service R&I files do. I made a mental note to double-check.

Hawthorn sipped his wine and smiled. "Continue."

"Well, then. Yesterday he took apart a health-food cafeteria over in Sector 68, up on Sunset."

"An android place?" Hawthorn asked.

"Yes, of course. He dismantled four yogurt dispensers and one realbread slicer. The whole floor was awash with prune flavor yogurt and soy wafers. Then he took the arms and legs off that big guy in the leopard skin who waits on tables. It doesn't make much sense, Vincent."

Hawthorn kneaded his wide forehead. "I'm thinking something. DBA-51, what's across the street from the dance hall on Main?"

"The Legal Procedures Center," I answered, faster than any human secretary would have.

"That health-food place is around 9100 Sunset, isn't it?"

Korngold nodded.

"Which puts it across the street from the State Employment Complex," I supplied.

Hawthorn's head bobbed and rings formed under his eyes. "Patterns, patterns," he said, bouncing up and circling the room. "What day is this anyway?"

"Wednesday," I told him.

He rubbed his bearded chin. "Why did I want to know that I wonder?"

"To see if perhaps this Dismantler strikes only on workdays?" I suggested.

"We can't tell yet," said the police captain. "He only started up on Monday. If he knocks off after tomorrow we'll know he's working a four-day week."

Hawthorn paced a triangle on the vinyl rug. "Something, something."

Captain Korngold asked, "Do you see any pattern in these screwy actions, Vincent?"

"The mind," said Hawthorn, "is like a . . . "

"Labyrinth," I supplied.

"The mind is like a labyrinth, Captain. We're like what's-his-name with the string the girl gave him. We're looking for the string to lead us out."

"So?"

"Right now I'm still in the labyrinth."

Captain Korngold's wrist rang. "Yeah," he said, answering his comphone.

Hawthorn slid toward me and whispered, "Is it time for any of my pills?"

"My eyes always light up when it is."

"I forgot that."

"Hell!" The captain shot to his small feet. "He's struck again."

"Who?" asked Hawthorn.

"Well, The Dismantler. Want to come along and look at the scene of the crime?"

"Am I," asked Hawthorn, "going to have trouble collecting my fee on this? We had to bill Justice Hall twice on that Samson complex case."

Korngold held out ten hundred-dollar bills toward me. "I had to swipe most of this out of the Widows Fund, but here."

I hesitated.

"Take the money," said Hawthorn.

The twenty-four-hour nightclub in Sector 28 was cluttered with android parts. It made me feel queasy. Hawthorn was on his knees in the midst of a scattering of dismantled waiters. He blinked his round eyes and let his forefinger circle his beard. "What am I doing down on the floor?"

"Looking for clues," I prompted.

"Have I found any?"

"You noted something written across one shirt front."

The word *Justice!* had been lettered in tomato paste across a waiter. Hawthorn stood, wiping his oil-stained hands on the legs of his dark suit. "Huh," he said and moved to the front window of the dim little place. On the top of the coin piano was a naked girl android. This one was a platinum blonde and a little harsh for my tastes. She was still dancing. Hawthorn made a fist and hit her in the knee and she stopped.

While Captain Korngold talked to his men, who were in turn questioning the two plump club owners, Hawthorn pressed his nose against the window beyond the piano. "What time did they say he struck here?"

"Eleven this morning."

"Same time, same time." He ticked his head, then said, "The building almost lost from view over there."

Without looking I told him, "It's the State Marriage Bureau."

"Something," he said.

"What?" At times it's fascinating to watch the human mind work.

"The time now is?"

"Nearly two in the afternoon."

"Don't I play tennis someplace every Thursday at this time?"

"Today is Wednesday. You go swimming at your club in half an hour."

Hawthorn put his flat palm over his beard. "Call a cruiser. I'll go swimming. Meet me back at the apartment at four. I'm getting a hunch on this case."

The smog darkened and cruiser lights blossomed outside the three-foot-square picture window. I used my right forefinger, which can serve as a corkscrew, to open a chilled bottle of white Pismo Beach '22.

When Hawthorn came hurrying into the apartment, almost walking sideways, I said, "Been swimming all this time?"

"I remembered I had a lunch date. Swimming is good for your memory. Though four o'clock is pretty late for lunch now that I think about it."

I poured a little of the Pismo Beach. "What of The Dismantler case?"

He tried the wine, scowled. "Bad. Too many clams in the soil up there. Throw that out and bring me some Laguna pinot."

I fetched the new wine. "Do you sense a pattern yet?"

"The violence, the scrawled word," said Hawthorn. "There's a strong flavor of revenge. And frustration."

"You think?"

"The location of the three places is significant," said Hawthorn. "Always across the street from a government office. What would frustrate you about those places?"

"The three in question, Legal Procedures Center, Employment Complex and State Marriage Bureau, are among the most difficult to deal with. There is a great deal of circumlocution."

"Exactly," said Hawthorn. "If you set out to call on a specific part of one of those buildings, say at nine in the morning when they open their doors, by eleven how far along would you be?"

"Not very. You'd still be in a pre-waiting room probably. Or at best in one of the actual waiting rooms." It's a painful fact that many androids simply don't function as well as I do.

"Each of those three administration buildings is staffed almost entirely by machines and androids," said Hawthorn. "But if you went to one of them, bent on revenge, chances are you wouldn't even get near an android in your first couple of hours. You'd have to, with a low patience quotient, rush out someplace else to take out your frustation. To the nearest open android joint."

"Usually right across the street."

"This," announced Hawthorn, "could be a Monte Cristo complex."

"Meaning?"

"Somebody feels he's been wronged by a certain number of government bureaus. Maybe he's even been sent away, transported in a manner he thinks unjust. Dumped onto one of the planet colonies. He returns, sets out to revenge himself on those responsible for his troubles. Like the Count of Monte Cristo did once he got the dough. Except this guy can't even get at those he's after. He settles for substitutes. Now then."

I sat ready to search my vast memory banks.

Hawthorn stood up, paced. "Find me all the people you have records on who have made complaints against the three bureaus in question. Either themselves or through legal counsel. Find me those people and what other bureaus they've had run-ins with."

I closed my eyes and whirred. "Um," I said. "Eleven thousand of them."

"Toss out those who aren't in the area at present. Zero in on those who've recently returned to Greater L. A."

I hummed for a second. "Nine hundred some names."

"Get me the ones who answer the description of this Dismantler."

I said, "Fifty-one of those."

"Get yourself tuned in on a phone circuit and check alibis with Captain Korngold's Alibi Squad."

This took almost an hour, since the squad is half human-staffed. While I was at the job, Hawthorn drank wine and then took to practicing his tennis serve. Finally I said, "Three possible men who have no, according to the GLA hidden monitoring system, alibis for the times in question. A Frank Amnar of Sector 35, a Walter Reisberson of Sector 24 and an Alfred B. Meskin of Santa Monica Sector."

"Give me their backgrounds."

"Meskin is the only one who's had a run-in with any other bureau besides the fatal three," I said. "He was sent to Mars for two years by the Space Placement Bureau. His attorney claimed at the time Meskin had merely gone in to apply for a job as a golf instructor at a Mars Canal Zone resort. But instead Space Placement transported him as a chimney sweep."

"Huh." Hawthorn had put on his tennis clothes while practicing and he tapped a bare knee now with his racket handle. "What were Meskin's gripes with the other places?"

"Legal Procedures Center, he claimed, made a mechanical error on his family inheritance. Putting a decimal point wrongly. So that he inherited $21 from his Uncle Ned instead of $21,000. LPC denied it and Automated Appeals backed them up. As for the Employment Complex, it seems Meskin was a golf instructor in the Laguna Sector. The EC called him in for retesting and personnel guidance and decided he was better suited to be a shop steward in a soy bean plant in Pasadena." I paused. "The State Marriage Bureau really did slip up. That was admitted at a later hearing but by that time it was too late since Meskin had been transported to Mars. The Marriage people misread the punch holes on his marriage license and sent his bride to a woman's prison farm near Oxnard."

"And he's returned to L.A. just recently?"

"Yes. He became a caravan outfitter on Mars after he bought himself out of the chimney sweep job. It's easier to change papers and classifications on a wild frontier place like Mars. Meskin got back to Greater L. A. on last Saturday with a half a million dollars."

"The rigmarole," said Hawthorn, swinging his racket, "is what drives people off the track. What's across the street from the Space Placement Bureau?"

"An automated supermarket."

"If Meskin goes to SPB tomorrow and tries to attack the androids who shipped him off his patience may

again run out at about eleven. Call Captain Korngold
and tell him to meet us at that supermarket at eleven
tomorrow."

I trailed along behind our self-propelling shopping
cart.

Hawthorn, his hands locked behind his back, was
studying the displays of wine. "Ugh," he said, noticing a
bottle of Venusian port.

Over in another aisle Captain Korngold gave an odd
cry. It was hardly eleven, a little early for The
Dismantler. I stopped and in a moment the captain
came over to us smelling strongly of chocolate cake.

"The damn bakery bins are on the fritz and spraying
everybody with aroma. They got one old lady smelling
like a Boston cream pie," he said. "It would have been a
lot simpler to grab Meskin at his hotel. Except he hasn't
been there for four days."

I said, "Meskin is here." I had sensed it.

The head of a pancake syrup android salesman came
flying over the wine shelves. "Yas, suh," it said as it
crashed into a display of mock avocados.

We ran along the slick aisles.

A middle-sized man, about thirty-five and with brown
hair, was scrawling *Justice!* on the breast of the giant
rubberized turkey which sat above the turkey-roast
display. He was using chocolate syrup he'd scooped
from an overturned icecream wagon. "Two years on the
wilds of Mars in cramped chimneys and worse!" the
man shouted. "My wife shucking corn in the pokey!"

This was Alfred B. Meskin, the man Hawthorn had
rightly deduced was suffering from a severe and
thwarted Monte Cristo complex. As we stood, a stunned
trio, Meskin grabbed an electric screwdriver from the

tool kit strapped to his wrist and went to work on a sausage-demonstrating robot who happened to be passing by. Meskin had made a fine flying tackle and now he set to work uncoupling the spatula arm of the prone machine.

"Rigmarole!" Meskin cried. "Round and round!"

Silently Captain Korngold drew his stunrod from his hip holster. "Come along, sir." He stepped over to Meskin.

Meskin made a brief attempt to dismantle the captain's left leg but realized he was a human just as the rod put him to sleep.

After the Police Service cruiser had taken off with Meskin, Hawthorn wandered back into the supermarket.

"You figured things out correctly," I said. "And named another new complex."

Hawthorn frowned. "What was that Captain Korngold smelled of?"

"Chocolate cake."

"We'll buy one," he said.

✿ The Yes-Men of Venus

INTRODUCTORY NOTE: Let me begin by expressing my thanks to the executors of the Arthur Wright Beemis Estate for choosing me to complete his unfinished stories, of which this is to be the first. Like so many others I have long been an admirer of the books of the venerable fantasist. Nothing has ever given me the thrill that reading his first novel, *Roo-So of the Jungle*, in installments of varying length in the old *Thursby's All-Star Electrical Fiction Weekly* did. Unless it was reading the twenty-three sequels, especially *Roo-So's Revenge* and *Roo-So, Friend of Animals*.

This present story belongs with Beemis' planet adventure yarns. It was in the winter months of 1929 that Arthur Wright Beemis penned the first of his many scientifiction novels. In an era when space travel was little known or speculated on Beemis had his likable two-fisted hero, Hyacinth Robinson, travel between planets with ease. Hyacinth Robinson, as you may remember, had been standing too near a reservoir in upstate New York and when the water evaporated he went with it, eventually drifting to Venus where most of *Vandals of Venus* takes place. This story was an instant hit and was soon followed by *Vagrants of Venus, Mermen of Mars, Misfits of the Moon, Plundered on Pluto* and many more.

Now that many of Beemis' books are freely available, it was felt by his estate that his unfinished work should also be given to the public. So here is the new Beemis we have all been waiting for.

Chapter 1: A Minor Cataclysm

My heart was heavy as I drifted over the remote reaches of the Pacific Ocean in the atomic powered Zeppelin the World League of Peaceful Governments had thoughtfully allowed me to borrow in order to show their gratitude for my having ended the Fourth World War several weeks ahead of time with my lucky discovery of a powerful ray that made gunpowder ineffectual. This balloon cruise, as pleasant as it was, had been planned as more than just a dedicated scientific attempt to map the migratory routes of the Arctic Curlew. It was to have been, too, my wedding journey.

As I followed with my binoculars, the happily paired curlews flapping to warmer climes, I tried to think of some reason for the unpleasant turn events had taken.

When I had called for my beloved Joanna on the prior morning her father, the noted munitions tycoon, John Plunderbund Brimstone, had left, not his best wishes for a safe honeymoon but, rather, orders for myself and my Zeppelin to be thrown unceremoniously from the grounds. All my leaden heart could be sure of was that I would never again walk hand in hand with the handsomest, most athletic and yet feminine girl in the state of New Jersey. The thought of what I was doing would have brought tears to my eyes had I not been as masculine and manly as I am. For the curlew was the one bird that my Joanna and I had always thought of as *our* bird.

But the rapid deflation of my Zeppelin vanquished all self-pity from my mind. I was galvanized into action. Placing my binoculars back in their case, I dived without further thought from the gondola of the falling Zeppelin and into the placid waters of the Pacific Ocean. Perhaps some well-placed parting shot from one of the minions of Joanna's father had done its slow work and been the cause of the untimely cessation of my means of transportation.

I am an excellent swimmer and so there was no dread on my part of the long swim ahead. However, I had barely covered a mile when I became aware that something was tugging rather forebodingly at my ankle. My impression was that I had caught my foot in the compelling maw of some great clam. Before I could reflect more the creature had pulled at me so forcefully that my head, the hair of which I wore in a somewhat long though manly fashion, was yanked below the breath-stopping waters of the ocean in which I had so recently found myself. I fought bravely, being an excellent boxer. An old ring axiom has it that a good big

man can beat a good little man. However, most rules of
honest boxing were not made with giant clams in mind.
For one thing, I could not be sure if I was fouling the
creature or not. As I struggled I became more and more
lightheaded and giddy. As I drove an excellent jab home
to what I hoped was a vital spot of the clam I suddenly
lost consciousness.

Chapter 2: The Mysterious Host

I came to in a clean white bed with a large handsome
man looking down at me. He was a striking fellow. To
give you some idea I will simply say that this man,
whose name I soon learned was Lowell Hawthorne, was
even better developed and more manfully handsome
than myself.

"You've had a bit of a close shave, old man," he said,
gripping my shoulder in a perfectly manly way.

"American, aren't you?"

"Right you are, old man," he said. "Mabu, my native
boy, and Numba, his native boy, fished you out of the
briny. Scared the simple fellows a bit at first. They're
not used to finding chaps such as yourself inside giant
clams. I had some talking to do to convince them you
weren't a large pearl or some such thing."

"I believe it is oysters rather than clams that are best
known for their pearls," I said, good-naturedly, for I
took to this handsome, though mysterious, American
almost at once.

"Who can tell a native anything?" was his honest
reply.

"I suppose I am to be laid up here for a time," I said.

"A few days," said Hawthorne, drawing a bamboo
chair near to my side. "If you don't object I'd like to

tell you a few of my adventures. For, if I do say so myself, my life has been both curious and strange."

"By all means," I encouraged, being anxious to learn more of this enigmatic man who apparently lived contentedly here among savages and giant clams.

"I can tell by your look," he began, "that you are a man of science and that you may at first be a bit skeptical. Let me begin by saying that for the past five years I have been in close radio contact with a man living inside the planet Venus."

"Inside?" I asked. "Come, Hawthorne. Science is well aware that people live on the outside of that damp junglous planet. But inside?"

"Put aside all your scientific learning for a moment," my new friend replied. "If you do you may learn something. At least you will have whiled away your convalescence."

So he began the odd and compelling narrative that you will read in the next chapter.

Chapter 3: Down and Out on Mars

I am the reincarnation, began Hawthorne, of an Egyptian priest, whose name if I were to mention it you would recognize as being as familiar to you as your own. Having lived several lives I reached this one with more than the usual sense of ennui. I tried many things, shopkeeping, the cavalry, gold prospecting, writing for the magazines. None of these helped, nor could love. For in ancient Egypt I had loved a handsome and sporting priestess named Isis. After her all other women were anticlimactic. As Fate would have it, she whom I sincerely and respectfully loved never seemed to get reincarnated during the same era as myself. You know how women are about keeping appointments.

One evening toward the end of 1970 I was strolling through Central Park long after the hour when most men thought it safe. To a man such as myself, a man who fought the Red Indians without a qualm, the worst terrors of Central Park after dark held no dread. Still I was taken aback when seven youths fell upon me with baseball bats. You have perhaps found, as I did that night, that even a superb physical being is no match for seven men with little respect for the correct way of life, and large clubs. Though I maimed and injured a good number of them I was nevertheless knocked unconscious.

When I awoke and took a step I bounced twelve feet into the air.

Some reappraisal of my surroundings seemed in order. Central Park had surely changed considerably. It was now a great red desert. I took another step and bounced again. Then the awesome truth came home to me. I was no longer in Central Park. I was on Mars.

I am aware that you scientifically inclined chaps talk of space travel as being a remote possibility. You will realize, of course, that in 1970 no such thing was even at the experimental stage. Therefore I knew I had been transported to the Red Planet by some mystical means there is no way to explain.

I was still engrossed in seeing how high I could bounce when three large green men rode toward me mounted on gigantic hairy horses that boasted two extra sets of legs. The green men themselves were twenty feet high and turned out to have, now that I noticed, an extra set of green arms. This is not the sort of sight someone who has only recently been battered with wooden clubs wishes to see on awakening.

But appearances are not always the best indication of the man and I soon found my green welcomers to be quite decent. By means of a method too complex to burden you with we soon taught each other our respective languages.

The green men were named Yarl Zun, Zin Yerg and Yex Zurb. I explained to them that I had apparently transmigrated to Mars by some strange means.

"You picked a bad time to transmigrate," said Yarl Zun, shaking his great green head.

"Why is that?"

The three of them proceeded to explain to me as we shared a breakfast of kex, which is rather like our cold oatmeal, that Mars was in the midst of a great depression. It seems that the head of their government, the Daktor, who is roughly equivalent to two of our presidents, had been wooed into the camp of the more radical element in the Martian society and instead of listening to his Yax-Daktors, or well-wishers as we would call them, and building up comforting supplies of zugbeams, or what we would call deathrays, he had foolishly poured the taxpayers' money into Yerb, which is something like our social security. The result was rampant radicalism and poverty with little or no respect for Goomba, roughly equal to our patriotism.

The upshot of the enlightening political indoctrination was that I would have a tough time making my way on Mars at the moment. Zin Yerg and the rest helpfully offered to bat me over the head with Zoobs, roughly equivalent to our baseball bats, in the hope that I might then transmigrate back to Earth. I, though, having been an optimist in nine out of ten of my previous reincarnations, decided to brazen it out. Stick I would and albeit I was down and out at the moment I felt I would not be for long.

Such was indeed the case, as I will next relate.

Chapter 4: The Great Games of Maroom

I threw in my lot with the green men who were, it evolved, en route to Maroom, the capital of this country, to enroll in the Great Games. It is difficult for me to find a parallel on our own planet for these Great Games. What transpired at them, as I was to learn only too well and shortly, was this. The bloodthirsty citizens of Maroom flock to a large stadium and there witness various fellows fighting one another and also great and ferocious beasts, of which there are many on this depression-torn planet. Should a poor mendicant triumph in one of these gruesome contests he is awarded a cash prize. This explains why the down-and-out of Mars flock to Maroom.

To Maroom then my new friends and I made our way. For, although on Mars I was now called Yar Sud, or Shorty, I still vowed that I would beat any man or beast I came up against in fair combat. Especially if there was money involved.

We had hardly reached the suburbs of the great and decadent capital when I heard a girl screaming in a tone that indicated her very honor was at stake. Borrowing a sword from Yex Zurb I jumped from my riding position just to the rear of his saddle and ran toward the scene of the struggle.

My green acquaintances had informed me that the green men were not the only race on Mars. There was also a pink-skinned human type much like myself only taller. Still I was not prepared as I dived into the murky, sward-choked alley between two crumbling ruins to see before me a girl of striking beauty of figure being pummeled by a large pink man in a leather suit.

"One kiss is all I request," the man pleaded in a slimy voice that was far from manly.

"One will lead to another," the girl responded in a tone I admired. "Soon you will require other favors."

"One little kiss. By Zarg [their idea of God]! If you don't kiss me quickly, Dina Taurus, I will have you locked away where kissing is out of the question."

"Lock if you will," said the brave girl. "For kiss you I never shall."

I waited to hear no more. "Stand, sir!" I cried. "The young lady does not wish to be kissed."

The man was nearly eight feet high, though it was evident that his pursuit of physical gratification left little room for a careful program of physical fitness. "Beat it, Yar Sud," he bellowed. "Do you dare to interfere with a Yax-Tarkas on his appointed rounds?"

"I don't know what a Yax-Tarkas is," I replied. "But I know that my blade will cut you down if you don't depart this woman's side at once."

His only reply was an angry grunt. He then came at me with sword drawn. In my student days in Paris I had astounded my teachers with my ability as a foilsman. Fortunately, on Mars they fence in the Parisian manner and I was soon able to run the pleasure bent Yax-Tarkas through and then dispose of his body in a pit beneath the ruins.

When I returned to the heavy-breathing girl I suddenly gasped. "Isis!" I cried. For she, indeed, it was.

"My name is Dina Taurus," she replied. "I do thank you for aiding me. For your kind act, though, I fear you will incur the wrath of all Maroom."

"My own Isis," I continued. "Whom I have not seen

for nearly two dozen reincarnations. Don't you remember me? Have you forgotten Egypt, my love?"

"You speak, sir, of love," the girl said in a tender
voice. "I was about to bring up the topic myself. I feel
somehow that even though you are shorter than most
you are a man I could someday marry and kiss freely. I
fear I have never met you before."

"Look, look," I said, beginning to draw a map of the
solar system in the dust of the alley with the tip of my
recently engorged sword. "Look there." I proceeded to
explain where the planet Earth was in relation to Mars
and then where Egypt had been. I told her of our great
love on that spot. "No wonder I haven't been able to
find you again," I concluded. "You've been rein-
carnating here on another planet. Be that as it may, Isis,
we are together again."

"As you talk and as I look at your handsome face it
comes upon me more strongly that I am fond of you.
Isis, however, I am not. Dina Taurus, a simple shopgirl,
is who I am. As Dina Taurus I sincerely hope you will
find your way clear to love me."

She was my own Isis and yet she had no recollection
of it. I determined to court her under whatever name
she was using. Once you have loved a woman such as Isis
it is hard to shake the habit. "Dina Taurus you shall
be," I smiled. "Dina Taurus, I love you and ask your
leave to pay court to you."

"My leave you have had since the moment you leaped
into this fetid alley," she replied tenderly. "Tell me, by
the way, what is your name?"

"My name is Lowell Hawthorne."

From behind us a grim voice spoke, "Lowell Hawthorne, we take you prisoner in the name of the City
and County of Maroom."

A dozen heavily armed men had approached us quietly while we had talked of love. "What is the charge?"

"Killing a Yax-Tarkas and throwing him in a pit. Come along with us."

To my new-found Dina Taurus I whispered, "Just what is a Yax-Tarkas, my love?"

"The talent agent for the Great Games," she gasped as the lawmen carted me away.

That is how I came to be sentenced to fight in the arena of Maroom.

Chapter 5: In the Dungeons

My cellmate in the dark stone room under the arena was a handsome tanned man named Joel Lars. We soon became fast friends, not merely because we were padlocked together but because we shared a great community of interests and also believed in the manly virtues and a planned program of daily exercise.

"We will not be called into the arena for many days," Joel Lars told me.

"Unfortunate," I said. "For I have only now remet a girl for whom I have searched many centuries on many worlds."

"Too bad," he replied with real sympathy. "Speaking of girls, would you care to hear my story?"

"It would help pass the dark hours here."

"It took place on Venus, which, as you may know, is a planet in this system of ours."

"I am a great admirer of that planet," I said. "Please to continue."

"Of the overall surface of that planet I know little," went on Joel Lars. "Of its interior I know only too much. For it is there that the only woman I will ever love, Virl Yank, is at this moment a captive of the fiendish Yes-Men of Venus."

"How does she happen to be inside Venus?" I asked.

"Let me go back a bit," said Joel Lars. "My parents were missionaries and one fine day they took their spaceship to Venus. Our crewmen proved disloyal and in a dispute over shorter hours they threw my beloved parents and myself over the side. We were stranded in the steamy jungles and my parents soon succumbed to the moist living. I, a mere boy of seven, survived and was raised to manhood by the Boogdabs, what the Martians would call Yarznigs, roughly equivalent to the Earth's great apes."

"What of the cursed Yes-Men and your dear Virl Yank?"

"Being raised by great apes had a strange effect on one," answered Joel Lars. "It took several years of therapy to completely rid me of the idea that I might be an ape myself. I still dream sometimes that my mother was. Now, as to the Yes-Men."

His narrative was cut short at this point by the arrival of a group of guards who pulled us to our feet. "There has been a last-minute cancellation," one of them, a coarse hairy fellow, explained. "The star gladiator is ill and you two will have to go on in his place."

CLOSING NOTE: What transpired next would fill a book itself. And this is exactly what my agent has advised me to do with it.

✿ Keeping an Eye on Janey

The small blond man looked across the desk at him and said *"The Shadow Bride of Ledgemere."*

Barry Rhymer poured himself more coffee from the gourd shaped carafe his wife had given him and said, "What?"

Shrugging with one shoulder, Bernard Hunzler repeated, *"The Shadow Bride of Ledgemere."*

Barry turned to watch the smudged brick walls outside his office window. "Excuse me, Bernard, I was thinking about something else. Yes, I like the title. Did I mention Flash Books has a new policy about our

Gothics? Now all we editors have to have an outline before we can request an advance. Just a couple of pages I can show to our business people here."

Hunzler asked, "Why? Look I'm Bernadette Austen, the queen of Gothic terror. I told you the title. Now give me the $1500 advance and I'll go home and write the thing."

"We have a new treasurer."

"I've written twenty-seven of these things for you, Barry. I helped make the Gothic revival the terrific thing it is in the 1970s," said Hunzler. "Now you do this to me. Listen, *The Shadow Bride of Ledgemere,* a Flash Books Gothic Special by Bernadette Austen, the Acknowledged Queen of Horror Thrills. Give me the money."

Barry said, "Tell me the idea while you're here and I'll have it typed up for you, Bernard. Best I can do."

"I promised Mother I'd buy her a rabbit-skin coat by the end of 1976," said Hunzler. "Here it is the middle of 1977 and she's still freezing her ass in the Bronx."

"A couple of pages to show our business people. I'm sorry. It's a new policy." Barry's desk phone rang and he flipped on the view screen and took up the speaker. "Yes?"

"I can," continued Hunzler, "go right over to Crack Books and say *The Shadow Bride of Ledgemere* and they'll hand me fifteen hundred bucks before you can blink." He grinned sadly, shifted his rimless glasses to a new position on his nose.

On the plate-shaped phone screen a heavy-set man with a head of short cropped gray hair had appeared. "Hello, Barry Rhymer," he said. "It's Gores of Gores Investigations here. You wanted to talk to me about the case we're working on for you?"

"Can I call you back in a few minutes?"

"I'm on a tail job right this minute," Gores told him. "I'm calling you from the 53rd Street branch of the New York Public Library while the pigeon is inside leafing through picture books on Etruscan art."

"You have a nice eye for details, Mr. Gores," said Barry. "I have someone with me. Just a second."

"An investigator is no good if he doesn't pay attention," said Gores. "I could have put a mechanical tail on this guy but I like to have personal contact. I used to pound a beat, 87th Precinct, back in the late sixties and it gave me a permanent taste for outdoor detective work."

"Bernard," said Barry, "this is a private conversation. Wait in the reception room."

Hunzler stood and pointed at the dictation typewriter under the other window of the narrow brown room. "I'll dictate my plot into that while you're talking. When I'm creating I don't hear, so you don't have to worry." He went and seated himself at the machine. *The Shadow Bride of Ledgemere,*" he said into the activated mike.

Barry hesitated, then spoke to Gores in a lowered voice. "It's about the mechanical operative your detective agency has in our home, Mr. Gores."

"He likes to be called Carnahan," said the agency head. "We go along with our mechanicals. Little individual quirks are what make the Gores outfit superior to most. What's the problem?"

Hunzler dictated, "Emily Frazier's mother and father are killed in India and she must fend for herself in the harsh competitive world of nineteenth-century London. It is, therefore, with a sigh of relief that Emily Frazier notes in the daily press of the period an advertisement seeking a governess for the two deranged sons of the lord of a mansion in the remote seaside town of Ledgemere."

"Well," said Barry to the detective, "your Carnahan is getting too aggressive, Mr. Gores. You know, I only wanted him to, well, you know."

"See what your wife was up to while you're in the city earning your livelihood," said Gores. "And that's exactly what Carnahan has been doing and is doing. A damn competent job."

"I'm wondering if I really need such bulky equipment. Originally, you remember, I asked for something compact. Postage-stamp-size maybe."

"All that type of stuff can't give you the details Carnahan can. It doesn't have his judgment, nor his compassion. You get one of those bugging devices the size of a grain of sand and it's got brains and heart to match." Gores looked back over his shoulder. "There was a fad for that stuff in the early seventies, but most sensible operatives are back with the heavy hardware again."

"Maybe," said Barry.

"Carnahan, believe me, is ideally suited to sit out there at your house in Harborland Estates, Long Island, and keep track of your wife and her carrying on."

"Okay, okay," said Barry softly. "But Carnahan keeps talking lately about taking a more active part in what's going on. He may, I don't know, speak up or do something physical."

"He does have those little hands and a concealed pistol built in for emergencies," said Gores. "I'll let you in on something, though. Carnahan is programmed to feel a little tougher than he really is. In these divorce cases you need an operative who thinks somewhat hard-boiled."

"It's not," said Barry, "a divorce, Mr. Gores. I love

Janey. I only wanted to find out what she was doing."

"You found out," said Gores. "She's sleeping with the top Mafia man on Long Island."

Barry winced, glanced over at Bernard Hunzler. Hunzler, his eyes nearly closed, was saying into the mike, "What then is the dark secret of the third floor of the strange house at Ledgemere? Why are certain rooms shuttered and barred? Why does the Victorian plumbing work no better than it does?"

"Naturally," continued Gores, "Carnahan's blood boils when he sees this Wally Rasmussen visiting your wife while you're here toiling in the canyons of commerce."

"This guy Rasmussen," said Barry, his lips hardly moving, "is not actually a top Mafia man, Mr. Gores. He's associated with the Amateur Mafia, which is that new crime syndicate that started in the early seventies. They're more liberal about who can join, take in non-Italians and so on."

"Who told you that?"

"I read it in *Newsday*."

"Yeah, well, Mafia or Amateur Mafia, he's a punk; and a hood in any case."

Barry said, "I admit that. Still, I don't want Carnahan doing something obtrusive. He just gets the facts and I take the action."

"What are you planning to do?"

"I haven't enough facts yet."

Gores' head snapped suddenly to the left. "There goes my pigeon. Looks like he just boosted four high-priced coffee table books on Etruscan art. Don't worry. Our chief computer is always in phone line contact with Carnahan. We'll have a talk with him. Bye-bye." The screen blanked to its usual rose-white.

"Thus it is that Emily Frazier emerges from the shadows at long last," Hunzler was dictating. "She can walk the proud halls of the mansion and be the true bride of Ledgemere for once and for all." He waited for the machine to finish typing and punched it off. He grinned another sad grin over at Barry. "That's worth more than $1500. The scene where the grave robbers burn down the grange hall is going to be terrific."

"Okay, I'll try to get a check out to you by early next month. Still at your mother's address?"

"Where else?" Hunzler left and Barry went back to watching the bricks.

Janey, a long lean girl with slim tan legs, dropped a servomechanism and said, "Damn. That's the third servomechanism I've dropped since breakfast. Not my day, Barry."

Barry bent and swept up the scattered cogs and springs from the kitchen floor with the side of his palm. He got all the parts of the broken coffee grinder gathered into his cupped hands and then dumped them into the repair chute.' "Maybe you can join me for a martini. Relax before dinner."

"The martini mixer is one of the servos I broke," said his tall blond wife.

"Oh," said Barry. Above the whirrings of the kitchen he could hear the surf hit the beach far below Harborland Estates. "I guess then I'll take a shower now, change."

"I could make you a drink by hand," said Janey. "I'm good at things like that."

"If you'd like."

"Would you like me to?"

"Sure, if it's no trouble."

"There's no trouble taking trouble for you." Janey hugged herself and her breasts huddled closer together. "Honestly, Barry. Why can't you be more direct? Assert yourself. You're thirty-one."

"Thirty," he corrected. "What do you want? Would you like me to come home and act like some wild Viking out of a Flash Books barbarian novel?"

"Better that than some Bernie Hunzler heroine," said his wife. "Better than moping around like poor little Emily Frazier going out to Briarcliff Manor to look after two deranged kids."

Barry said, "Wait. Say that again."

"You don't have any balls."

"No, I don't mean the essence. The specific words."

The slender blonde said, "I was referring to Bernie's book before last that I proofread when you had the flu. *The Shadow Bride of Briarcliff.*"

"Christ," said Barry. "I just bought the same Gothic novel twice."

Janey said, "Who'd know?"

"I don't want to have an argument."

"So don't."

"I buy us this damn place where you can actually hear the Long Island Sound." He waved in the direction of the beach. "You might as well face things, Janey. *The Shadow Bride of Briarcliff* helps pay for that ocean." He rose up on his toes, sighed and spun around. He aimed himself at their bedroom and went in there.

The bed said, "Dames are like jungle cats. You have to treat them rough."

"Shut up," said Barry. He closed the room's laminated door and shook his head at the kingsize bed. He noticed a wisp of smoke coming up from the rug. "Hey, are you on the fritz?"

"Relax, sweetheart," said the bed's hidden speaker grid. "I'm enjoying a gasper."

"A what?"

"A cigarette. Your pal Rasmussen left a pack of bootleg coffin nails behind and I just set fire to one and am having a drag. Sometimes when I'm alone here time can seem as lonely as a football stadium in the off-season."

"Smoking in bed is dangerous." Barry sat down, slumped, on a lemon-yellow lounge chair. "I don't know, Carnahan."

"I know," replied the bed. "Knowing is my business, sweetheart. There's not a dame alive you can trust."

"Keep your voice down." Barry tilted and unfastened his shoes. Moving across the rug he reached into the bathroom and started the water roaring in the shower stall. "Was that guy here again today?"

"You ought to read my reports more carefully," said the bed. "Rasmussen is almost always here, sweetheart. Unless she's there." A slight gurgling came from beneath the disguised listening machine.

"What else have you got under there, Carnahan?"

"Rasmussen also left the good part of a fifth of bourbon behind."

"You're actually programmed to drink, too?"

"I'm not a cop, sweetheart. I can drink on duty." His voice was taking on a bit of a brogue.

"I thought Janey never liked bourbon," Barry said. "I keep trying, Carnahan, to come up with some mutually satisfying solution to this situation."

"Sometimes," said the surveillance device, "lead is the best solution."

"Lead?"

"Bullets talk louder than words," Carnahan told him.

"Let's get something straight. I'm more than just another bugging device. Sure, I can tape conversations, film assignations, collect data on adultery. But the New York State law is such at the moment that evidence collected by a bed is not admissible in a divorce action. So I give you the dope I gather and you have to decide what to do. I can have opinions, though, sweetheart." He apparently took another drink.

"You guys, you and Gores, are always talking about divorce." Barry paced from the bed to the open bathroom. "I never said anything about separating from Janey."

"Don't lump me with Gores," said the bed. "He's only my partner."

"Gores is your partner now? Come on, you're nothing but a monitoring device."

"I might even go into business on my own some-time," said Carnahan. "I'm getting tired of these divorce cases anyway. They leave a bad taste in my soul. I'd like to work outside more."

"You'd look great trailing somebody up 53rd Street."

Carnahan exhaled cigarette smoke. "This caper may get cut off sooner than you think."

Barry strode back to the bed. "What does that mean?"

"There's a contract out on Rasmussen," said Carnahan. "The real Mafia doesn't like the way the Amateur Mafia is cutting in on things here in Long Island. They're going to hit Rasmussen."

"You mean kill him?"

"Cancel him in lead," said Carnahan. "Make him a candidate for the hoodoo wagon."

Barry said, "I hadn't seen anything about the rivalry being that intense."

Carnahan said, "And you won't read anything in the papers about the torpedoes who were parked across the street."

"Gangsters across the street?"

"Most of this afternoon, sitting in one of those little electric sports cars," the bed told him. "They're not the boys who'll make the hit, just a couple of gunsels staking Rasmussen out for Giacomo Macri's Mafia family. Outside talent will be brought in for the real kill job."

Barry said, "You're telling me that Mafia people are parking around outside our house in little electric sports cars and plotting to kill Wally Rasmussen?"

"Little red electric sports car."

"No, they wouldn't try to kill anybody in Harborland Estates."

"Death doesn't have much class sense, sweetheart."

Barry put his palms flat on his chest. "But Janey might get hurt."

Carnahan said, "She may not be the best dame in the world, but she's a good kid at heart. Nothing's going to happen to her while I'm around."

Barry wandered toward the bathroom. "I'll do something."

"Yell copper?"

"Not the police yet, no. They might make more of a mess than you and Gores have. I'll have to talk to Janey."

The bed dropped the bourbon bottle. "Oops," it said. "Okay, have it your way, sweetheart. You're the client."

"Another thing," said Barry. "My agreement with Gores states you're supposed to turn yourself off and not record when Janey and I are here. And I don't think you're keeping all your mechanisms well enough hidden under there. Janey's bound to notice you when she makes up the bed."

The bed chuckled. There was a faint click and Carnahan stopped talking.

Walking into the bathroom, Barry stood around.

The folding chair unfolded itself when Barry activated it, setting itself up on the sand. The copy of the weekend edition of *Newsday* flashed its headline when he tossed it into the chair. *Prominent L.I. Hood Gunned Down.* Barry had read the story already, found it wasn't any of the prominent hoods he knew about. Gulls were sitting out on the buff-colored rock near the shore. He turned from the headline and stood trying to concentrate on the brownish birds.

At the water's edge Janey, in a one-piece black jersey swimsuit, was rambling in the shallow water. Barry set his lips in a firm position and was about to stride to her when he heard something in the thick brush of the hillside behind him. He turned. A wide swath of twisted bushes and scrubby grass was being agitated as something low and wide descended from above. Barry checked on Janey and saw her bend and skim a white pebble across the quiet water. He walked up toward the rattling underbrush. He jogged when he got to the rough path leading back toward their sea-edge home.

"The ocean looks like a great reservoir of sadness," said Carnahan.

"What in the hell are you doing out here?" He hopped off the path and into the bushes. Carnahan was in there, tilted way over to the left and smoking a cigar.

"I just got a tip from a stoolie the Gores computer knows," the bed told him. "This is a hot tip."

Barry looked up toward the backs of the other three houses sharing this stretch of beach. "Have you been drinking bourbon again? Coming out here in the middle of the morning. Somebody's going to see you." He put a hand against the footboard and gave a tentative push.

"People are used to odd things in the suburbs, sweetheart," said Carnahan. "Get this straight now. I just heard that Giacomo Macri has hired a couple of boys from Detroit to hit Rasmussen. It's going to happen real soon."

Barry stopped and put a shoulder to the redwood footboard. "Okay. Now go back uphill."

"That's a real Maxfield Parrish sky today, isn't it?" remarked the big bed. "I've got to get more outside work."

"When are these guys going to do it?"

"All I know is soon."

Barry said, "I'm going to talk to Janey right now."

"Okay, sweetheart. I won't take the play away from you yet." Carnahan grunted, made a high-pitched whirring sound.

"They're going to hear that, somebody is. What's wrong?"

"It's tough to get traction in this sandy ground."

Barry put his shoulder to the bed and after a moment of straining Carnahan's wheels took hold and he shot forward and began rolling, rattling, uphill and away.

The gulls on the rock all took off when Barry neared Janey. "You scared the birds," she said.

"Janey," he said.

"Now what?"

"Sometimes," he said, "we're judged by the company we keep."

"True." She ran two fingers of her left hand along her

thigh, then picked up a pale orange pebble with the toes of her left foot and flicked it into the foam of the ocean.

"What I mean is, sometimes when we play with fire, if you'll forgive the cliché, we sort of get burned, as they say, I guess."

"Also true. So?"

"Well," said Barry, glancing at Connecticut across the water. "There's a lot of crime around these days and it's a problem."

Janey frowned, her lips parted. "Listen, Barry."

"Yes?"

She shook her head. "Nothing, never mind." She walked away from him, out into the water.

He hesitated, didn't follow.

The doctor's face faded from the phone screen on the living room coffee table. "Dr. Lupoffsky says it isn't," Barry called toward the kitchen.

Janey brought him a container of self-brewing tea and placed it on the table. "Isn't the Brazilian flu again?"

"I thought I had a relapse. But this is the Argentine flu."

"At least it's still South American. What are you supposed to do?"

"Same as with Brazilian flu. Stay home from work a couple of days, drink fluids," Barry said. "Do I look particularly green to you, by the way?"

"No," said his wife. "Should you?"

"Dr. Lupoffsky said the only thing that worried him was the green tinge to my face."

"He says that to all his patients," said Janey. "The color reception on his phone is out of adjustment."

The phone sounded and Janey flicked it on. Bernard Hunzler appeared on the screen. "Barry there, he's not in his office they told me?"

"Barry is sick today, Bernie."

"Only take a minute, Jane," said the Gothic writer. "Hey, Barry, can you hear me?"

"I'll take it," Barry said, gently pushing Janey away from in front of the phone screen. "Yes, Bernard?"

"Can't we salvage *The Shadow Bride of Ledgemere*, Barry? Make it a series. The Gothic adventures of Emily Frazier." Hunzler grinned and his eyebrows drooped.

"No, we don't want a new series at Flash Books right now. Just change the names and the plot and resubmit the outline."

"I was hoping to get the $1500 right away. I've got to buy mother the electric blanket."

"I thought it was a rabbit coat."

"She broke her hip over the weekend and she's confined to bed."

Janey pulled the red cellophane tag on the tea cup and the tea began to steam. Barry said, "Change the names and the title, Bernard."

"*The Shadow Towers of Woodville*," said Hunzler. "How's that sound?"

The front door of the house was pushed in and two men in tan jumpsuits stepped over the threshold. They had net stockings with paisley patterns pulled over their faces. One aluminum revolver was in the gloved right hand of each man. "Okay, Big Wally," said the man moving into the room. His stocking mask was sky blue.

Into the phone Barry said, "Call the police."

"What kind of title is that for a Gothic?"

The other gunman, the backup man, jerked the phone

cord from its baseboard slot. "We got no orders on the dame. Just you, Rasmussen. We hit here after ten, when the schmuck who lives here is at work."

Janey swallowed. "He's not Wally Rasmussen. He's my husband."

"Into the bedroom, lady," said the man with the sky-blue mask.

"I'm not Rasmussen," said Barry. "Her husband is home sick today. It's me."

"Sure, sure, Rasmussen," said the other gunman. His stocking mask was fire pink. "Look, you're dealing with the real old established Mafia here. We aren't amateurs. Giacomo Macri set this all up perfect. He even used a computer. Bam, we fly in, bam, we hit you, bam, we go back home on that new Penn Central train. It's lovely."

"Look at him," insisted Janey. "Does he look like Rasmussen?"

"Sure. A little greener than in his photos, but more or less. Well, not that much maybe but we haven't got time to fool around. We're already one bam behind."

"Didn't you hear him say Macri used a computer on this," said the other masked man. "Those things don't make mistakes. Rasmussen is supposed to be here weekdays after ten, so this is him. You want to be gunned down standing or sitting, Big Wally?"

"Okay, punks, grab some ceiling," said a harsh, faintly Irish voice. The bedroom door was swinging open. "Drop the roscoes and reach." Carnahan, still unmade and rumpled, rolled up to the opening. From beneath his box springs two black .45 automatics were pointing.

"Who's under there?" asked the fire-pink gunman.

"The name is Carnahan, sweetheart. Drop the rods."

The man let his pistol fall, but his partner did not. He dived to the side and started firing at Carnahan.

Carnahan's two automatics roared at once with a tremendous sound. The gunman was hit in the left side, but he kept on shooting. The big bed was having trouble squeezing through the doorway. He had to tilt himself up partially sideways and that put him at an awkward angle. The wounded gunman put four bullets into Carnahan's underside.

Barry had jumped up at the first shot and rushed Janey across the room, down on the floor and away from the shooting. "Into the kitchen," he told her now.

The masked man who'd given up his gun grabbed it up and ran for the front door as Carnahan began shooting again. "This isn't going as programmed," he said as he left.

His partner got off one more shot at Carnahan's still exposed mechanism and followed out the front door.

The living room was sharp with the scent of gunpowder. Barry waited for a moment, then stood. "You okay, Janey?"

She hugged herself, said, "Yes. You?"

"Seem to be."

Carnahan gave a rasping cough. His voice was dim when he asked, "Hey, are you two kids okay?"

Barry approached the bed. "I'll get you unstuck and we'll have you repaired, Carnahan."

One of Carnahan's automatics dropped from his retractable metal hand. "No, sweetheart, it's too late for repairs. Too late for tears. I figure I can kiss tomorrow goodbye."

Janey got to her feet and came toward her husband. "We have some talking to do, Barry," she said. "I'll call the police now."

"No," Barry said. "We'll talk first, then call the police."

"The big sleep," said Carnahan. "The big sleep." He made a low ratcheting sound and ceased to function.

Hobo Jungle ☼

Inside the guitar were a blaster pistol, an interrogation kit and two chocolate bars. "Any emergency," said the Head of the Political Espionage Office, "any small emergency, and you reach into the back of your guitar."

Lt. Ben Jolson of the Chameleon Corps said, "I was wondering why it had such a strange tone." He took one of the chocolate bars and slapped the secret compartment shut.

"No," said Head Mickens, "the tone is authentic, Ben. We even had the computer over in the Folklore Bureau listen to the guitar."

Jolson, tall and lean, in subdued civilian clothes, said, "What did Tunky Nesper say?"

Head Mickens blinked and his forehead crinkled. "Who?"

"Nesper, the one I'm going to impersonate."

"Oh, we didn't think to ask him," said the Head. "He's a thousand miles from Keystone City anyway, way on the other side of Barnum in a rehabilitation center. I think we can safely trust our folklore computer."

Unwrapping the chocolate bar, Jolson said, "Okay, what's the exact assignment?"

"You have," said Head Mickens, "a certain hostility to computers, to machinery in general, Ben. I did slightly myself until I went to that robot analyst. He cured me of my hypochondria just like that." He patted the top of his desk, touching photos of lizards and stacks of railroad schedules.

"What are you taking pills for now then?" Jolson seated himself in a copper-colored chair and took a bite out of the candy bar.

Mickens' eyes widened slightly and the dark spots beneath them lowered toward his cheeks. "It's hay fever season. I really have that. Wait till you get to Murdstone. The pollen count on that planet is fantastic. Three hundred fifty on a good day and anything over ten is trouble."

"I don't have hay fever," said Jolson. "Murdstone? That's where the Political Espionage Office is sending me?"

"Yes," said Head Mickens. He stopped looking for his medicine and held up a photo of a brownish lizard man wearing a velvet suit, a flowered vest and with a large red stone stickpin in his full tie. He was posed next to a silver bicycle, his bowler hat held in one scaled hand. "Erdon Swaffle, the President of Lagunitas Territory on Murdstone. Lagunitas, as you probably know, is a somewhat backward area. The landcar is just appearing there, air travel is unknown, and the economy is still heavily based on crops and cattle, though there is an expanding, but primitive, industrial system."

"Lizards run the place," said Jolson.

The Head found a punch card memo. "The population is roughly half lizard people and half human types. Fifty-fifty, though the giant lizards dominate and control." He located a spool of micromagazines, then noticed his hay fever capsules beneath it. "Excuse me a second. These are tough to swallow without water, aren't they? There. The government of Lagunitas Territory is democratic but, apparently, corrupt."

Jolson pointed at the microfilms. "I read those articles about the Lagunitas government that Tad Dibble did for *Muckrake.*"

"Exactly what I was going to show you." Head Mickens let go of the spool. "Here's the problem. It seems there's a big suitcase buried someplace in Lagunitas with $1,000,000 in cash in it."

"Embezzled?"

"Yes," said Mickens. He sniffed, almost sneezed. "Dibble has learned that certain officials in President Swaffle's cabinet, especially the Secretary of Nutrition, have been siphoning funds for the past two years."

"Their funds or Barnum money?"

"Ours. Barnum's. Much of this hidden money appears to have been taken from the various welfare funds Barnum distributes on Murdstone."

"This wasn't in the articles."

"No, Dibble has been in contact with Political

Espionage Office agents on Murdstone," said the Head. "Which is what initiated, in part, your present assignment."

"Why is the million in a suitcase? Why didn't they spend it?"

"Oh, they spent two million," said Mickens, sneezing. "This is an additional million intended, apparently, for getaway money. Our Barnum government would like it back, but we can't openly ask for it. The government of Lagunitas is too shaky." He held up a picture of a plump green lizard in a tufted smoking jacket, who was sitting at a white marble table and enjoying a slim black cigar. "This is Linol Zee Bemsher, multimillionaire newspaper publisher and mineral heir. He lives on his own island and is pretty conservative. The Political Espionage Office has suspicions he might attempt a coup if Swaffle's administration teeters much more than it is now. He'd be worse."

Jolson crumpled the candy wrapper and tossed it in the floor dispozhole.

Mickens said, "Now, here's what you have to do. You become this fellow, Tunky Nesper, this drifting folk singer. He hasn't been on Murdstone in a couple of years, but they all know him. He comes and goes on all our planets and arouses no suspicion. He drifts from planet to planet, picking up songs, doing odd jobs. He probably needs therapy. That's his problem, though, not mine." The Head sniffed, sneezed. "Dibble, the reporter, is working on a story undercover. He's in a little rail town in the biggest agricultural valley in Lagunitas. You slip in as Tunky Nesper, find out from Dibble where the money is hidden."

"He knows?"

"Yes. You find out."

"Then steal it back."

"Right, and arrange to get the stuff out of Lagunitas Territory." Head Mickens felt some more of the things on his desk. "You won't have any trouble changing into this Tunky fellow?"

Jolson had the rare ability to change shape at will, to impersonate anyone, many things. He'd been processed by the Chameleon Corps, during a dozen long years at the Corps Academy. He'd gone in young, not quite in his teens. Then the Chameleon Corps had seemed to offer an adventurious life as well as a secure profession. That was twenty-one years ago. "No, no trouble," said Jolson.

"The guitar-playing may give you a little trouble."

"I already know how to play the guitar."

Head Mickens said, "So you do. I read so many dossiers in a day I forget whose attributes are whose. We do have some gadget they can implant in your brain and it gives you the ability to play the guitar. Or any musical instrument, for that matter."

"What," said Jolson, "happened to the idea that I was semiretired from the Chameleon Corps?"

"You are," said Head Mickens. "Now I realize we discussed the idea that you'd only have to carry out a minimum of assignments for PEO in any given year, Ben."

"Three," said Jolson. He was slouched slightly in the chair.

"Three, four," said the Head. "Verbal agreements don't have much influence on the Barnum government, Ben. After the next elections maybe. You know how the Chameleon Corps is set up. Because of the monumental amount of time and money involved in creating one single agent, CC can't ever allow one to quit completely."

Jolson said, "By the way, during my last assignment

two hundred dollars worth of stuff in my ceramics warehouse got broken."

"There's a check being put through on that," said Mickens, massaging his cheek bones. "The payment has to come out of the Office of Public Works."

"Why?"

"I made the mistake of mentioning that some of your statuary was broken, and they mixed it up with a request for a new life-size statue of the Unknown Commando for the Keystone marina. Don't worry." Mickens sneezed. "I know you'd like to devote yourself fulltime to your ceramics business, Ben. Espionage has to take priority. The number of critical situations in the Barnum System is growing. I have a chart showing that, here somewhere. Jagged black line going up and up."

Jolson hunched, stroked the side of his neck a few times. "I believe it even without graphic proof. Where do I find this muckraking reporter Dibble?"

"Sleep-briefing has all the addresses and phone numbers and the rendezvous-point stuff," said the Head of PEO. "Wait now. There's another fellow I should mention. Older man, also a crusading journalist and a political cartoonist. He lives in Lagunitas Territory somewhere or other. Human type, big lump of a man with gray hair, wiry. Punches people in the nose a lot." He held up a news photo. "Henry Carlos Barby, prize-winning newsman and artistic journalist. He's supposed to be sympathetic to our Barnum government. PEO uses him as an information source. You might keep him in mind."

"Any passwords or countersigns to use with him?"

Mickens said, "He doesn't like that sort of thing. No code phrases and particularly no numerical identification phrases. He took a poke at our last man when he tried numbers on him. He doesn't even have an

address number. A real individualist. You'll just have to
look him up and say hello."

Jolson stood and picked the weathered guitar off the
Head's desk. "How long do I have on this assignment?"

"Depends on events, on what you encounter."
Mickens blinked. "Still, could you have the money at
the spaceport in Peralta Territory by a week from
tomorrow?"

"That's the territory next to Lagunitas, isn't it?"

"Yes, the nearest spaceport. Barnum doesn't allow
one nearer, since Lagunitas has a Backward Territory
rating. Let us know when you'll have the money there.
You think you can bring it off in a week?"

Jolson said, "We'll see." He opened the guitar and got
the other chocolate bar out.

The lizard smiled, bit down on his cigar and resumed
his piano playing. His left hand played heavy clumpy
rhythm and his right a tinkling, skittering tune. On his
bright green head his derby bounced and his tail flicked
in time. "If I send for my baby," he sang in a sandy
voice, "man, and she don't come. If I send for my baby
and she don't come." He shifted his cigar, continued.
"All the doctors in Zaragata Station sure won't help her
none." He left off singing but the piano rumbled on.

Jolson was in a wooden chair at the table nearest the
piano. He had one sinewy hand around a schooner of
needled ginger beer. He was Tunky Nesper now, sharp
featured and weather worn, wearing a much-washed
work tunic and trousers. He looked to be in his middle
forties, perhaps a few years more. His eyes were an
intense blue, watchful but slightly tired. He had sandy
red hair, thin and curly. "Don't quite scan," he said to
the lizard man.

"Um, um," said the pianist. He was watching the

keys, seemed to be looking for the end of the tune. "Zaragata Station is hard to fit into a lyric." He stopped playing, glanced at the glassless window in the small one-room wooden saloon. It was afternoon outside, bright hot.

There were three other customers in the place, human types, wearied dusty men in work clothes. The lizard used his tail to spin himself off his stool. "Anybody want a refill?" He was also the bartender.

The men, each at a different lopsided table, all shook their heads no.

The lizard stretched up and walked over to join Jolson. He pointed at the guitar. "You must be Tunky Nesper."

"Don't see no use denying it," said Jolson in a flat nasal voice. "Though sometimes I get to thinking I'm just a clump of dumler weed, blowed by the wind."

The lizard's cigar had gone out and he relit it with a wooden match. "Heard of you. I guess you've been every place."

"Every place twice," said Jolson. "And elsewhere, too. Rolling like a ball nobody throwed."

"Down around Woodville, in the hobo jungle, they sing a different version of that song I just did," said the lizard man, removing his derby and resting it in his lap. "You ever heard it?"

"I've heard lots of things," said Jolson. I've heard things I wanted to hear and things I didn't. Heard men dying for no reason, and dark winds blowing people's houses away and money being made."

From another table a gritty man said, "You talk pretty poetic for a bum."

Jolson took his guitar from his back and made room for it atop the off-kilter table. "We're all of us bums, brother, hoboing through life. All of us. I remember once around Railcross Center I met a guy thought he wasn't. But he was."

"Lots of words," said the gritty man.

"This is Tunky Nesper," the lizard told him. "You must of heard about him. I wouldn't mess around."

The man had started to rise, sat again. "That's who he is? Yeah, I've heard. I've heard he knows how to fight like nobody else. Excuse me."

"Well," said Jolson, swinging the guitar to his back again, "I know how to fight and I know how not to fight. All depends."

The lizard man placed his derby on the table top and tilted it toward Jolson. Inside where the label should have been was a slip of bag paper with the numbers 13-15-24-1-18-15-2. "Where you heading from here, Tunky?"

"Where my feet take me," said Jolson. "Where the wind blows me to. Don't much matter. Who you are is more than where you are. I been thinking about just hoboing, hitting the jungles between Zaragata Station here and Woodville. Haven't been on Murdstone in two years and more, nor around the Zaragata Valley." In a much lower voice he added, "20-14-7-15-2."

Puffing on his cigar the lizard nodded. Outside on the dirt road, a horse-drawn wagon went by, piled high with dusty potatoes. "Railroad detectives been getting tougher with most of the jungles. About ten miles out of Zaragata Station there's a little stopover station called Thorneville, and back in the woods the hobos got a good place, still pretty safe."

The gritty man said, "I'd like to see somebody smash all this."

"Careful now," said the lizard. "Don't go talking

against the railroads and the farm owners. Not out in the open when you don't know who you're with."

The gritty man snorted. "Smash it every which way for all I care. I only worked ten days out of the last thirty. Keeps up, I'll have to hit the Welfare Store in Woodville. Or go live in one of the poverty camps in the woods."

"Watch out for those," said a blond-bearded man. "They're recruiting from those."

"Who is?"

"Anybody who needs hands free," said the bearded man. "Get you fined and then put you lining track or picking tomatoes to work it off. Or they send you down to Penny's Farm, the prison farm, and you're working for the territory for thirty days."

"Ought to smash it all," said the gritty man.

The third man, plump and red-speckled, said, "You two guys get my dander. Guys like you. Look, I work every day I want to and I don't tell nobody to go to hell and I even paid taxes once. You guys and this so-called Hammitty bastard, they ought to put you all to work on Penny's Farm for good. Do some honest work and stop bitching."

"Smash you, too," the gritty man told him and threw his lopsided table. Its edge caught the plump man in the chin, and one of the leg tips poked hard into his stomach.

Jolson said to the piano player, "Will I find Dibble in the hobo camp near Thorneville Station?"

"He's waiting there, calling himself Keystone Slim," said the lizard man. "Use your numerical sign and countersign stuff. Excuse me now. I have to stop this before the town militia or the railroad cops come in." He ran and grabbed the gritty man from behind.

Finishing his ginger beer, Jolson made his guitar more

secure and dived out a side door. Dust was blowing south along the railroad tracks and he headed with the wind.

The leaves turned black as the day ended. The last of the sunlight snapped away and it was abruptly night. Jolson worked his way down through the tree-filled hillside, tangling with brush and vines and thorned wildflowers. A trace of cook smoke was coming on the warm wind, drifting up from below him. Insects began clicking and whirring, birds called and sang all around. Jolson's guitar made a whacking sound and struck against the bole of an orangewood tree. He back-stepped to dislodge the instrument, and when he moved ahead again, a fist hit him low in the chest.

Another hand, not a mate to the fist, slapped tight over his mouth. Somehow his feet left the ground and he was moved downhill and through a gully and into a bowl-shaped clearing. When they put him on his feet and pushed him toward the single large campfire, Jolson said, "That's what I like about being on the road again. It makes life run over with mysteries and surprises."

There were some fifteen people scattered around the fire, five of them lizard men. There were two women with the group and no one who resembled Tad Dibble, the reporter Jolson wanted. He grinned his leathery, faintly sad Tunky Nesper grin and unfastened his guitar. Standing next to him was a slim girl in a gray work-singlet and gray trousers. He tossed the instrument to her and said, "Obliged if you'd watch this." He spun and faced the two hoboes who'd waylaid him. "I been hoboing since I wasn't no bigger than spit. Seems to me you two are about the unfriendliest fellows I've seen in a while."

The bigger of the two had a wide-brim brown hat, no

shirt, and checkered pants tucked into a pair of high
lace-up boots. "We stop everybody. This ain't no
welfare store, welcome one and all."

"That I know," said Jolson. He moved up to the man,
then pivoted as his blue-coated companion slipped a
knife out of his pocket. Jolson chopped the knife out of
the man's callused hand. Reached for him.

"Hold on, hold on," said a lizard from the other side
of the fire. "All that talk and that short temper. This
fellow has got to be Tunky Nesper. I heard he was on
Murdstone again."

The brown-hatted man asked, "You him?"

"Far as I know," said Jolson.

"I'm Kid Brown and this is my partner, Raincoat
Ziegler." He held out a big hand.

Jolson shook it. "Now I know your name, it makes
me sort of sentimental. I'd feel bad now if I broke your
arm."

"All my fingers are sprained," said Raincoat. "Otherwise I'd shake hands, too. We've all heard of you,
Tunky."

"Yeah, I'm like the drought," said Jolson. "Lots of
people have heard tell of me."

"We caught a tamis and we already had five pounds
of potatoes fell off a wagon," said the lizard man who'd
recognized Jolson. "We've got stew enough for everybody."

"I forgot," said Raincoat, whose major garment was a
frayed kneelength coat with military buttons. He
reached three tomatoes out of his coat pocket with his
good hand. "I swiped these on the way here."

"In the pot, and then you two get back to standing
guard," said the lizard. "Come on over, sit down,
Tunky."

"I feel I will," said Jolson. "Seems like I been walking

since I was half-growed." He sat on a log near the lizard man. "Things in Lagunitas Territory look worse. Everybody getting tougher?"

"Things always look worse," said the lizard. "I'm Woodville Shorty." They shook hands and he said, "President Swaffle and his cronies keep running things worse and worse, and there's been more riots in the big towns and the city. Makes everybody restless and low spirited. These kind of times lots of people like to crack heads. Jobs are tougher to find, too. And the railroad agents are making it harder to ride."

"Seems like every time a fellow tries to stand up for himself, two other fellows come along and want to knock him down."

The lizard man grunted up. "I have to look after the stew. We'll eat in about a quarter-hour."

The girl with Jolson's guitar walked over and sat next to him. She had chestnut hair, long and hanging below her shoulders. She was hardly twenty, with a face just too thin. She was pretty still, but sad and tired. "Here's your prop," she said. Her voice was soft and careful.

"Thank you." Jolson took the instrument and dropped it to the moss at his side. "Me and this guitar been through a lot of long and lonesome nights, a couple of leaves blowing anyplace."

"You sure have that crap down," said the girl. "Must be a strain not to wince. You say them like you're embroidering each one. I had an aunt with crap like that all over her walls. She raised me, trying to use the maxims to get her over the hard parts."

"Well, now," said Jolson, "some folks talk a lot and some not at all. There's people who favor each style."

"You can relax with me. They all believe you're who you say. Dibble's not here any more."

Jolson said, "Oh, so?"

"Keystone Slim to you." The fire crackled up and her face flashed bright and clear for an instant. "15-14-22-20-24-22-11," she said.

It was one of the identifying phrases. Jolson gave the proper response, then asked, "And who the hell are you?"

"Sarah," she said. "That's enough name for now. Dibble found out something new, that someone may have moved what you're looking for. He took off three days ago, for the Pinero Woods."

Jolson swung his guitar up and rested it on his knee. "Are you with the Political Espionage Office?" he asked quietly, while tuning the guitar.

"No, I'm real," said Sarah. "I'm just drifting. I was born on Murdstone, not in this territory."

"How come you know what Tad Dibble was up to?" Jolson tried a few chords.

"I was sleeping with him."

"Okay," said Jolson. "Three days he's been gone. Is that what he expected?"

"No," said Sarah, "he should have been here by yesterday. He planned to check out a lead in one of the poverty camps and then return in time to meet with you today."

"You know exactly where he went?"

"Yes, I can take you there," said the slim girl.

"Would it be safer to travel there at night?"

"Yes. After dinner things will settle down to cards and drinking. We can move out then."

"Won't you need to rest first?"

"No," said Sarah, "will you?"

A whistle sounded and oil lanterns blossomed in the woods above the gully.

"They got by the lookouts," shouted the lizard-man

cook. He and the other hoboes kicked dirt on the fire.

"What?" Jolson jumped up.

"Railroad police," said the girl. She caught his hand. "Come this way." She pulled him away from the dying fire and straight across the camp site. "In between the white pines."

Jolson followed on the run. Back over his shoulder he saw lizard detectives coming down through the brush, derbys on their scaled heads. The yellow clubs in their fists were swishing through the cold black air.

The slim girl bent and stretched, scooped a palm full of water from the narrow stream. She drank, wiped her mouth with her wrist. "Downhill and out of the woods and we're there," she said.

Jolson squatted beside her. The night was thinning away and a chill dawn light was filling the forest. The trees were white and tall, close together and straight. "And Dibble didn't tell you what he thought had happened to the million?" He drank from the stream.

"No, I told you," said Sarah. "A man down there at the poverty camp has been giving Tad bits of information. He got word to Tad four days back that he'd learned someone had taken the money from where it was hidden." She sat back on her heels.

"But nobody knew where the stuff was hidden? Not this informant . . . what's his name anyway?"

"Mamlish. No, Tad had traced the embezzled money here to the Zaragata Valley from down in the capital, in Janela. Rumors of hidden money had been floating around for a couple of months. Only Tad and President Swaffle's gang knew."

"You say Dibble made sure the money was really gone?"

"Of course," said the girl. She stood, stretched.

"They'd had the suitcase buried under an old out-building some thirty miles uphill from Zaragata Station. There used to be a gold-dredging operation based up there. The suitcase was gone when Tad checked. He'd left it there so nobody would get suspicious until you arrived. Didn't do much good."

"Now I'll try," said Jolson.

As Jolson stood up, Sarah moved her slender face to meet his. "You guys, you PEO mercenaries, come in from above. You do your dirty stuff and get out. You don't have to give a damn."

"You could be right," said Jolson. He turned away from her.

"I only work here," said Sarah at his back. "Isn't that how you feel? That's what they say at the Welfare Bureau and at the prison farms everywhere. You don't give a damn who dies or who gets the crap kicked out of him and how many kids never grow up."

Jolson faced her. "Look," he said. "I'm here to get a suitcase with a million dollars in it. What I feel about how things are here and what you feel about how things are, isn't important now."

"Sure," said Sarah. "Nobody even has to see your real face. Tad has to put himself on the line, and he can get hurt."

"Let's find him then," said Jolson. He left her and waded across the stream. The sun grew warmer and the last of the dawn mist disappeared.

Halfway down Sarah caught up with him. "Drifters, we're like kids," she said. "I can ask any questions I want to."

Jolson hunched his shoulders, got his guitar to rest easier. "It's like the wind blowing through the pines is how I see it. Wind can go most anyplace, blowing free like it does."

The girl frowned at him, then noticed the two thin teenage boys off in the trees to their left. Sarah said, "We're friendly. Looking for Mamlish."

The boys nodded and Jolson and Sarah continued down toward the edge of the woods.

Malmish shook dry tobacco out of a biscuit tin and onto a cigarette paper. He was a dull gray color, almost fat. "They're all bums and trash here," he said as he rolled a cigarette. "I'm the only one in this whole community has an indoor toilet."

"Noticed that right off," said Jolson. He had an elbow resting on the glassless window frame of Mamlish's shack. There were nearly two dozen shacks built in the small clearing. One-room patchworks of crate wood, split rail ties, fresh lumber, flattened tin drums, squares of sacking and rounds of bottle glass. "Some folks seem like they can carry civilization around with them."

"Now," said Sarah, "where is he?"

Mamlish licked the cigarette into shape. "Why am I here in Lagunitas Territory at all? It's senseless. I had a home appliance store on Barnum, pulling down $20,000 a year. Then I go and fall in love and follow her here where they never heard of an electric can opener or a pop-up toaster. Even the millionaires, the lizards, they make toast in a wood stove or over the fireplace grate. They barely got electricity. All for love, that was me in my twenties. I'm only thirty-four now, but I look fifty. I spent over $40,000 on the wrong woman. How old do I look to you?"

"Thirty-four," said Jolson. "Where's Tad Dibble?"

Outside, a small child began to cry. "They're all like that," said Mamlish. "Always complaining. Either that or they're trying to figure some way to get back into the system. The best they can ever think up is another way of starving."

"Did he get here?" asked Sarah. "Stop all the crap and tell us."

"I never saw him," said Mamlish. "He never got here."

The girl watched him light his cigarette. "You're sure, Mamlish?"

"Yeah, I'm sure." He looked at Jolson. "Dibble pays me ten dollars for my items of info. This is all you get for nothing."

Jolson scratched his chin and narrowed one eye. He reached into his trouser slit and got a $10 silver piece. He walked across the scrap-wood floor and put it in Mamlish's hand. "Okay, now you imagine to yourself I'm Tad Dibble and you give me the details you been saving up."

"I heard a rumor from a couple of railroad dicks who got drunk in Woodville," said Mamlish, putting the money away inside his loose coverall. "They said somebody had a special railroad car hooked up on one of the expresses about a week ago. All that was put inside the private car was a big suitcase. I don't even think the railroad knew about it, not even the big lizards in the capital." He puffed at his cigarette. "That suitcase. I think it might be the suitcase Dibble's so anxious about. I've heard a couple other things, the source of which I'm keeping to myself, indicating such is indeed what happened."

"Maybe," said Jolson. "Where'd that private railroad car go?"

Mamlish laughed, shrugged. "It never reached the end of the line, never reached Janela. Someplace between Woodville and the capital that special car with that special suitcase inside left the track. I don't have any news about where."

"You really haven't," said Sarah, "heard anything about Tad?"

"Nothing," said Mamlish.

Sarah moved to the doorway. "I'm going to look around, ask around."

Mamlish shrugged again. "Makes no difference to me." He grinned at Jolson after the girl left. "These reporters run with some pretty odd women. I don't like bad language in a woman. This girl I followed from planet to planet never used a foul word."

Jolson said, "It's your forty thousand." He walked out into the dirt street. A woman in a flowered dress was hugging herself in the doorway of the next shack, watching him with only faint interest. He didn't see any sign of Sarah.

"Where you bound?" asked a thin black man who was seated on a crate in front of his shack.

"Well, now, I never much know."

"Where you been then?"

"I just come down from Zaragata Station."

"Any kind of work up there?"

"None I heard of."

"What I figured," said the man. He started to say something more, stopped. Nodded his head slightly, murmured, "Trouble."

Jolson heard horses coming and turned. From the forest to the left, three lizard men were riding. Two in tan uniforms and one in a frock coat and a bowler hat. "The law," he said.

Barely moving his lips, the black man said, "They're the ones took your friend Dibble."

"Hey, Red," called the lead lizard, one of the uniformed ones. He had a cluster of black dots next to his ear hole, and he scratched at them with a scaled green hand as he rode closer.

Jolson remembered he had red hair and replied, "Pleased to meet you, officer. You sit horse well."

"Let's see your papers, Red," said the lizard policeman.

"I'd sure hate to think there was some trouble getting ready to happen," Jolson said. He reached out his packet of fake IDs.

"Bring then over here," said the second tan-uniformed policeman. He reigned up on the other side of Jolson. His head was held stiff and only his amber eyes seemed to move at all. "Over here."

Jolson handed the papers in the near-leather wallet to the lizard. "My name is Tunky Nesper. Just drifting through, officer. Tumbling with the wind."

"You have a permit for that guitar?" the lizard asked, fingering the wallet. Its pebbled pattern was similar to that of his brown-green hands.

"Well, now," said Jolson, "you got me there, officer, because I been through Lagunitas more times than a one-eyed man can count and I never heard of a permit being needed for a man's guitar."

The civilian lizard's horse started to snort and dance, and the bowler hat fell from the lizard's head. The black man caught it and handed it up. "Your hat, Clerk Strangeby."

Clerk Strangeby got his horse under control and his hat back on. He made his mount canter up to Jolson. "I take it you're not on the way to gainful employment."

Jolson shook his head. "No more than dead leaves are being blown anywhere special, Clerk."

The clerk leaned forward, his hands stroking the pommel of his metallic saddle. His small, ridged nostrils fluttered and he smiled. "We'll put aside the usual proceedings with you, since I sense you're brighter than the average deadbeat."

"Well, that's fine," said Jolson. "You're a cut above the usual clerk, if I may say so."

"Yes," said Strangeby. "My job is to help these two officers recruit men to work down on Penny's Farm." He smiled again, and the smile seemed much older than he was, a dry, wrinkled smile. "The plums and nectarines are coming in two weeks early, and we need more men to pick."

"So you folks are out framing yourself a few extra hands."

"I don't think we need carry things that far with you, Nesper. Do you, men?"

"What then?" asked the policeman with Jolson's papers in his hands.

"Would you, Nesper," asked Clerk Strangeby, "like to help us out for only a week or so? Free room and board, indoor plumbing. We'll pay you a dollar a day on top of all that. You see, Nesper, if we trump up a charge, I'll have to sentence you to thirty days on Penny's Farm. This other way you make seven dollars and all you can eat, and in a week you're drifting again like, as you'd say, the wind through the woods."

"Am I right," said Jolson, "in figuring this Penny's Farm is a prison facility?"

"For some," said the clerk. "You have my word you'll be paid and allowed to leave at the end of our plum emergency."

Jolson puckered a cheek. "You the clerk of just the nearest town?"

"No, the whole county," Strangeby told him.

"Well, then I figure you can be trusted."

"You and I will shake hands and these officers will witness it."

"Only thing else a man could ask would be a seal with a ribbon stuck on a piece of expensive paper," said Jolson. If the black man was right, Dibble was probably already at Penny's Farm. This was a quick way to get inside the place. As he shook the lizard's cold hand he glanced around the shack town. Sarah must have slipped away into the woods.

"You're now doing business with Strangeby," said the lizard clerk.

"My pleasure," said Jolson.

When the bright sun was straight up over the orchard, the lizard overseer flicked Jolson across the back with his whip. Jolson, halfway up a ladder, went on picking red plums and depositing them in the bucket attached to the peg on his ladder.

"You snubbing me?" called up the lizard, flicking Jolson again harder.

"Oh," said Jolson, "I didn't realize you were being social."

"That crack of the whip means it's noon mealtime," explained the lizard. "Get those plums boxed and then fall in line for the march to the mess hall, Nesper."

"Seems like I haven't eaten since about the day after they invented food," said Jolson, climbing down.

The overseer moved down among the trees, cracking his whip at the other pickers.

Jolson grabbed his work tunic from a limb and, after

transferring the fat plums carefully from his bucket to a wood box, went down the lane between the fruit trees and waited with the half-dozen or so other pickers already there. Slipping the tunic gingerly on, Jolson asked, "Anybody know Keystone Slim?" He hadn't spotted Dibble in the two hours he'd been on Penny's Farm.

None of the workers, four human and three lizard types, answered.

Then a blue-green lizard shook his head at Jolson. "Literary criticism," he whispered.

"What's that you say?"

"They put Keystone Slim in the stockade," said the lizard man. "For literary criticism."

"How'd he come to get involved with that here-abouts?"

"You'll see."

The mess hall had only half a roof, the rest of it had apparently burned away in a long-past fire. Brown sparrows and bright cardinals hopped on the charred beams, chittering in the strong sunlight. A hundred men were at the long raw-wood tables. At each place a metal plate had been set out. Each plate held a boiled potato, a scoop of rice and a scoop of white corn meal, all under thin orange-colored gravy.

Jolson reached for his steel fork and said, "Well, that smells pretty good, when you compare it to the general odor of this place."

"Not yet," warned the blue-green lizard man, who was next to him. "Fold your hands."

"Is this prison farm run along religious lines?"

At the head of the dining hall, shaded by the existing section of roof, stood a fat, green lizard man in a fresh white suit. "I'm sure you're all anxious to find out what happens next," he said to the prisoners. "First, however, let me introduce myself to those of you who have just joined us today. I am Managing Warden Collis Enx." He paused, smiled a green smile at them all. "A name so far known chiefly to penologists and to scum such as yourselves. But a name destined, I modestly predict, to be a household word. Enx. 'Not since Enx,' critics will say, 'have I enjoyed a work of speculative fiction so.' Ah, but you grow impatient for your next installment." The white-suited lizard drew a thick manuscript from beneath his arm. "Some of you have come, cringing, up to me and have been kind enough to compare this present work favorably with my earlier, and unfortunately also unpublished, speculative novels. One fawning scoundrel among you told me he enjoyed it more than either *A Visit to the Future* or *Looking Around Technopia*. Well, though I don't intend to always be restricted to praise from scum, I am appreciative." He cleared his throat and turned to the midsection of the strung-together pages.

" '*A 100 Years Hence; Or, What Might Happen Tomorrow If We But Allow It*, a Work of Sociological Speculation by Collis Enx. Chapter VI: In the Bosom of the Future. With what trepidation I looked down upon the vista my ethereal guide had revealed by the simple gesture of reaching out one delicate hand and drawing back the metal-like material that in this curious world one hundred long years hence served for the manufacture of window curtains, as well as, I might add, lap robes, overcoats, blankets and some kinds of rugs and carpets, I cannot quite put into words. ' "

Aloud, Jolson said, "I got a feeling we're going to spend an awful long time getting to nowhere." He picked up his fork and pronged the potato. "I had a pet swink chased his tail just like this fellow writes. Round and round and the best it ever got him was a chunk of his own backside." Jolson ate the potato.

The blue-green lizard nudged him, whispered stiff-lipped. "I don't know what they call it where you come from, Nesper. But what you just voiced goes by the name of 'literary criticism' around here."

"I was hoping so," said Jolson. "I've picked about all the plums I care to on one assignment."

Managing Warden Enx's black eyes were watching Jolson, but he went on with his futuristic romance. " 'It seemed near incredible to me, as it does still, that in a scant hundred years the whole physiognomy of society as I knew it could be so incredibly transformed and transmuted.' "

"Seems like a man ought to be able to choose, even in prison, whether he wants to take his meals with or without literature," said Jolson in the completely quiet mess hall.

Enx snapped the manuscript closed, said, "You, you babbling outlander scum. There are two things I will not tolerate on Penny's Farm. Do you know what they are?"

Jolson ate a forkful of rice thoughtfully and then stood up. "Well, I know bad writing isn't one of them."

Enx started to throw his scientific romance at Jolson, but halted and got control. "No, you vernacular scum, the two things I hate are slow workers and literary critics. Guards, into the stockade with him. Grab him at once."

Three big lizard guards had already done that by the time the Managing Warden finished speaking.

Jolson caught his balance in the middle of the six

prisoners and said, "Right pleased to meet you all." The guards who'd chucked him into the low room were locking and bolting the heavy door from the outside.

The stockade room was about half as large as a boxcar and made of fitted planking. It was windowless. The hot light of the day fell down through a grilled opening in the low ceiling. "Don't go prancing all over my grandad," said a blue lizard man.

Jolson noticed now an old lizard man sprawled on the sod floor. "I always have a great respect for old folks."

"Respect for the dead is what's in order," said the lizard man. "Grandad passed on last night."

"Why don't you dig a hole and stick that old coot in it," said a gritty man, wearing only the bottom half of a set of thermal underwear.

Jolson said, "I do believe we met at the Zaragata Station saloon."

The gritty man replied, "Yeah, but I had clothes then. I got in another brawl right after you left and soon found myself here. Boy, I hope they smash this whole territory soon or I'm for sure not going to make it."

The bereaved lizard man said, "Without a church service, I'm not going to bury my grandad nowhere."

A fuzzy old man wiped sweat from his bare chest and said, "I don't like old dead relatives underfoot. It's not sanitary, spreads disease. We're going to all catch it."

The gritty man said, "He died from not enough food is my guess. We all got that already."

"I don't like you saying my grandad isn't sanitary," complained the lizard man. He had his wrist bandaged with a yellow neckerchief.

"Anybody who's dead isn't sanitary," the fuzzy old man told him. "When I'm dead I'll be the same. I have

nothing personal against your late grandfather, though
in the week I've been in this hole I found him to be a
pretty dull old boy."

A thin young man with sandy hair spoke to Jolson
now, "You look like Tunky Nesper."

"And a good thing I do," said Jolson. "Since that's
who I am. You look like a fellow named Keystone
Slim."

"Yes," said Tad Dibble. The left side of his face was
bruised and his lip had two black scars on it.

"Old home week has no place in a serious discussion
like we have going on here," said the lizard man.

"Why don't you just call the guard and have him give
your poor old grandaddy a decent burial outside
someplace?" said Jolson.

"I been calling since dawn and they don't pay no
attention." The lizard man tapped Jolson on the chest.
"Some of us have been in this stockade a while, buddy.
You just moved in and already you're trying to take
over."

Jolson smiled his sad smile. "Well now, I been tossed
and tumbled a lot, not handled with care, but I have
always managed to land right side up."

"Don't mess with him," said the gritty man. "He
talks poetry but he'll coldcock you. He's Tunky
Nesper."

The lizard man paused, shuffled back from Jolson.
"Oh, I didn't catch the name." He bent and caught hold
of his grandfather's body. "I'll drag him out of the way
so you and your newfound friend can talk."

Jolson guided Dibble toward the wall. "You okay?"

"They beat me up a couple times," said Dibble. "Out
in the Pinero Woods and here. Did they get Sarah?"

"No," said Jolson. "She's off and free. Have you thought that Mamlish might have put the police on you?"

"Yes, it's more than likely," said the reporter. "Did you try to contact Henry Carlos Barby yet?"

"The political pundit? No."

"Don't," said Dibble. "He's not on PEO's side anymore. Right after I told him I'd located the money, it was taken. I'm pretty sure, with Henry Carlos Barby's help, the money suitcase has been taken to Linol Zee Bemsher's island."

"The newspaper publisher," said Jolson. "His island's down the coast from here, off Low Harbor, isn't it?"

"Right, it's called Funebra Island."

"And where's Henry Carlos Barby now?"

Dibble sighed perspiration off his lips. "What's the date?"

Jolson told him.

"Barby should still be at his home, a big gingerbread mansion on the outskirts of Low Harbor. Day after tomorrow he'll be out on Funebra Island. Linol Zee Bemsher is having some kind of birthday gala for himself then."

"I'll have to get to Barby before then," said Jolson. "Take his place if possible."

"First," said Dibble, "you have to get out of here. Why are you in, by the way?"

"I heard you were."

"A tough way to set up an interview."

"We'll work out an escape plan," said Jolson. "What time do they feed us?"

Dibble said, "I've been inside this box two days and they haven't yet."

A new morning was showing through the roof slot when Managing Warden Enx came in carrying the guitar. He had on another white suit. He gestured at Jolson and said, "You can't imagine why I'm here, Nesper, you scum."

"Don't tell me you've set your novel to music?"

Enx's green fingers tightened on the neck of the guitar. "Ah, ah," he said at last. "An artist of my stature can't be baited." His tongue flicked out for an instant and his nostrils drooped. "Ironically, Nesper, it is your dubious art which is the subject of my visit."

"Art," said the gritty man. "What about food?"

"Come out into the fresh air with me at once, Nesper, or I'll withdraw my permission for this entire sorry business." Enx spun around and bolted outside.

Jolson nodded at Dibble, followed. The guards slammed the stockade door the moment he was free of the room. The flat fields all around flickered yellow; the fruit trees were thick with picking men. "Now," Jolson said to Enx's wide back, "what did you have in mind?"

"Over there," said the fat lizard. Under a barren tree, half covered with shade, stood a horse-drawn wagon. Stenciled on its side was ETHNOG: A DIVISION OF THE BARNUM SYSTEM FOLK BUREAU. "It seems our arrogant mentors on Barnum can come and go as they please, Nesper, and they have chosen to come to Penny's Farm and record you."

"Beg pardon, sir?"

"Record you, put your dreary rural wailings on some sort of cylinder so that it will be preserved," explained Managing Warden Enx. "So that useless dilettantes on Barnum may recline on lush upholstery and listen to your sod-kicking laments while true artists languish."

"I never said half as much against your work." The stenciled words on the wagon looked to be freshly painted. "Matter of fact, you got a nice style, but your plotting is a mite weak."

Enx thrust Jolson's guitar at him. "Take this and report to the wagon. I'm allowing you one hour, Nesper, to make your contribution to posterity. Then, I do think, it'll be time for a little literary discussion between you and me and a bull whip."

"Some folks just can't take criticism." Jolson ambled toward the shaded wagon.

The rear door, which still showed traces of the name Nolan's Wild Animal Show on it, swung open. "Come on, get your ass in here," ordered Sarah. She had on a tan jumpsuit and her chestnut hair was pulled back into double braids. ETHNOG was stenciled on the fabric over her left breast.

Jolson said, "It's like the warden was just now observing. You folks from the big city are a wild lot." He jumped up the hanging wooden steps and into the wagon.

"I've got to leave the door open, Sarah said. "Enx insisted. I had to sweet-talk him for ten minutes to get him to keep guards out of here." Her voice lowered more. "How's Tad? Is he all right?"

Nodding yes, Jolson sat on a wooden bench built under a window. "Right over there in the stockade. He's in pretty good shape. Yourself?"

Sarah's thin, pretty face had a smoky cast and her eyes were faintly red-rimmed. "Been awake most of the night, forging papers and filling out fake forms."

"Your idea to get in here this way?" Jolson rested his guitar on his lap and started tuning it. Loud he said, "Things sure tend to get out of tune in captivity."

"I had help, not much, from a Political Espionage Office agent, over in Woodville near the Pinero Woods. Fellow Tad had worked with. He got me some forms and papers to copy after I got the idea these guys would have to let a folk project inside," said the slim girl. "Ethnic stuff and spying, that's about all the attention Barnum pays to most of this planet. Your PEO buddy helped me round up the wagon and letter it." She moved to a hand-wound recording unit opposite Jolson. "He offered to sleep with me, too, but I told him I had too much forging to do. You work like that, too, make love to the girls you run into on your assignments?'.

"No," said Jolson. "But I can if you like."

She made a sour smile. "I've got to get Tad and you out of this place within the next hour."

"Shouldn't be hard," said Jolson. "I figure Enx, our gifted Managing Warden, can't keep himself away from here for more than a few minutes. If he does I can coax him over. When he looks in I can grab him. Take his place long enough to spring Tad, and the rest of those guys, from the stockade. Use his identity to get us through the gates and away."

Sarah's new smile was less sour. "Yes, that will work." She cranked the square, black recording box and aimed its pickup horn at Jolson. "Tad and I better stay out of Lagunitas Territory for a while. But you'll follow up on the money suitcase?"

"Right."

"We'll have to pretend to record something. Go ahead."

Jolson spit dust away. "Seems to me that songs are like bridges. So, to my way of thinking, the more songs we make, the more rivers we can cross. Why, if we make enough of them, there won't be nowhere we can't go.

This here first one I made myself, and it's entitled, *They Sure Hand Out a Lot of Crap Down on Penny's Farm.*"

He began to sing and Sarah turned away.

The six-foot-tall red-haired girl sprinted across the marble wharf and gave Jolson an enthusiastic hug. She bit Jolson's double chin, tongued his left ear, tugged at his wiry white hair. "Enough," said Jolson and set the giant girl aside.

"He's up in one of his warehouses and won't be out for hours," said the girl, who was lovely though big. "Not until he dodders up to the main château to dress for his party tonight."

"No doubt," said Jolson. The lizard boatman was watching the big redhead, and he bumped into Jolson and dropped a Gladstone bag on Jolson's foot.

The girl asked, puzzled, "Aren't you going to punch Seaton for that?"

"I'm most sorry, Mr. Barby, sir," said the lizard man, quickly tugging the suitcase off Jolson's foot.

Jolson, who was now a facsimile of Henry Carlos Barby, said, "Next time." He'd learned, during the few hours he'd spent with the real Barby, that the political writer and cartoonist didn't talk much. Even after Jolson had given him a shot from his truth kit, he couldn't get anything but short confessions out of the man. And before Jolson had given Barby a sleeping drug and hidden him in the attic of his rococo mansion, he'd heard nothing about this large, red-haired girl.

"Mr. Barby is being quite nice to you, Seaton."

"That he is, Miss Smith," said the lizard, touching his forehead with one scaly blue-green hand. "It's as my wife says, Miss Smith, you're a kind person. She reads your column in the *Times-Harquebus* and to her you're the only kitchen adviser who can write a recipe that touches the heart."

"Go away," said Jolson.

"Yes, sir."

The marble wharf turned into steps which led up the steep incline of Linol Zee Bemsher's private island. The stairway was wide and lined with marble urns. Each urn contained a different variety of poppy. Orange, yellow, scarlet, gold. The hillside that hung above the quiet blue water was thick with greenery. Shrubs, trees, fronds, ferns, all bright green in the noonday sun. "He won't tell Linol Zee anything," said Miss Smith.

"Better not." Jolson picked up his suitcase.

The redhead gave a sighing laugh and picked up Jolson. "I've got a spot all picked out in the North East greenhouse, Henry. Let's use that." She went bounding up the broad marble steps, cradling Jolson like a stack of firewood.

"Down," he told her. He figured she was F. P. Smith, who wrote "Heartaches in the Kitchen" for the Bemsher chain of newspapers. He'd been sleep-briefed to the effect that she was Bemsher's mistress exclusively.

"Am I being too aggressive again, Henry?" F. P. Smith reluctantly placed him on his feet. She popped her head forward and kissed his ear again. "I do like older men better than old lizards."

"Understandable." Everything around them smelled of rich flowers. "Money got here?"

F. P. Smith, who was wearing riding clothes and boots, said, "I don't want to talk about Linol Zee's schemes to conquer the Lagunitas Territory." She shrugged her broad shoulders. "This whole planet is just silly. Murdstone, indeed."

"Planet I love best." Jolson began climbing toward the crest of the hill. "Where is he?"

"I told you, Henry. Off with some part or other of his collection," said the girl. "It's pianos today, I think. My god, he has four hundred and eight of the damn things. We have a fulltime piano tuner now."

"Music is okay."

F. P. Smith caught up with Jolson and undid the ribbon in her bright hair. Shaking her hair free, she said, "Are you sulking about something, Henry? I think being mixed up in politics is making you awfully cranky."

"My profession."

She said, "How can you keep insisting that drawing those dreadful little pictures constitutes a profession? Like the other day, Henry, when you drew that pig and it had Zaragata Flour Trust lettered on its side. Whoever saw a pig like that?"

"Poetic license."

The red-haired girl ran up the last of the steps two at a time and beat him to the top. "Well, let's not argue, Henry. Let's use our stolen hours to better advantage." She sat and tugged off her riding boots, rose and flung them away into the foliage. "I want to abandon myself with you."

A lizard with a trowel and a gardening hat stood up in the brush where F. P. Smith's boots had landed. "It wasn't a serious blow you dealt me, Miss Smith." His left eye-ridge was cut.

"Oh, good morning, Fritch," said the red-haired girl.

"Morning, Miss Smith, Mr. Barby."

"Back to work," Jolson told him, and the lizard gardener ducked away out of sight again.

F. P. Smith strolled away down a graveled path and went into a great wrought-iron and glass greenhouse.

When Jolson found her, she was calling, "Are we alone in here?" through cupped hands.

No one answered.

She nodded, smiled openmouthed at Jolson, and pulled her riding blouse straight up over her head and off. "Over there under the lilacs, I thought. Does that meet with your approval, Henry?"

"One flower's as good as the next." Jolson dropped his Gladstone bag.

Marble houses were scattered across the island, some meant for living in and some for the storing of Linol Zee Bemsher's collections. As night fell, Jolson and the lizard publisher were on the sea facing open porch of one of the warehouses. Below, men and lizards in longboats and launches were scattering flower petals on the darkening water. "A little whim of mine," said Bemsher. He was already dressed for his birthday party, in a tuxedo and stiff white shirt. Fiddling with his ruby studs, he added, "Fresh-cut flowers teleported from Barnum, Henry Carlos. And see those yellow ones there, being tossed out now. California daisies. From Earth, Earth in the solar System. Picked this morning."

"Pretty," said Jolson, who was also in a tail coat and white tie. "Money safe?"

"Certainly, Henry Carlos," said Bemsher. "As a whim, a little whim, I have hidden it in a special place. Tomorrow, when I've recovered from tonight's fête, I'll take my private railroad car down to the capital and deposit the suitcase in my vault at the *Times-Harquebus* building."

"Where's the railroad car now?"

"At the siding near Railcross Center, right across the water from us. You should know that, Henry Carlos.

You're getting forgetful," said the lizard publisher. "I've been meaning to mention this." He reached into his coat's inner pocket, produced several political cartoons clipped from the newspaper. "See these, Henry Carlos. Last Tuesday you drew this pig with a top hat and labeled him Greedy Lettuce Interests. But the Wednesday before, look here now, a pig with a top hat is labeled Ruthless Traction Kings. Just yesterday here comes a pig in a top hat labeled Zaragata Flour Trust. Forgetful, isn't it?"

"No, different pigs."

"They look very much alike to me, to my senior political editor as well," said Bemsher. "And somewhere I have a letter of complaint from the Pig Growers' Association." A large splash sounded from below. "It's Mrs. Doob-Halprin. Always the first to arrive," said Bemsher, leaning far out toward the dark water.

"She fall in?" asked Jolson, who was reaching under his jacket.

"Her horse did," said the publisher. "I don't like her to bring him on the guest boat."

Jolson looked quickly in several directions, opened his truth kit, and pulled out a one-shot needle. He jabbed it into a soft sopt beneath the lizard publisher's ear. Bemsher's scaled hand made a brushing gesture, his knees buckled. "Easy now," said Jolson. He caught the big lizard man by the elbow, eased him across the marble porch, dragging him the last few yards. "Start telling me about the money."

"Barnum News Synd really did pay only $50 per cartoon for those reprint rights, Henry Carlos."

"Not that money," said Jolson. He pulled the publisher into the dark marble warehouse vault and propped him against a wooden crate marked BIG

LITTLE BOOKS: EARTH, 20TH CENT . "The embezzled money in the suitcase. Where is it?"

"Hot cocoa," said the publisher.

"What?"

"I like a hot cup of cocoa before I go to sleep, Henry Carlos."

"You're not supposed to go to sleep; you're supposed to tell the truth." It occurred to Jolson that the truth-kit needles might be mislabeled. "Where's the suitcase?"

"In the Warehouse 3 safe, Henry Carlos," said Bemsher in a drowsy voice. "Now be still and let me sleep."

"The combination?"

"You are getting forgetful, Henry Carlos. You already know the combination." The big lizard man rocked twice, plumped over on the gray-streaked marble floor.

Jolson hesitated, then scouted the room for an empty crate. He found one in a corner, tugged it back, and hefted the sleeping publisher into it. He replaced his studs and cuff links with Bemsher's ruby ones. When he left the warehouse, he was a reasonable duplicate of the lizard publisher.

There were acres of bright lawn, lit by flares and paper lanterns. Half a hundred tents of striped and colored canvas had been set up. Lizards in silk suits roamed the grounds playing violins. White-coated men passed with trays of imported pâté, ten assorted kinds of fish eggs, chafing dishes filled with cheese fondues, glasses of Earth champagne, tankards of dark Martian ale, Barnum soft drinks. A handsome old woman rode by on a wet horse. Several dozen guests had now been boated from the mainland. Plump lizards in white tie and tux, smoking cigars. Lizard women in bustled white dresses. Human-type men in opera capes and top hats, white gloves. Lovely young girls in fragile gowns, their skin dusted with eggshell-shaded powder.

"Happy birthday, Linol Zee," called Mrs. Doob-Halprin from her horse.

Jolson smiled, waved.

"Your flowers," said a young girl of eighteen with golden hair, "are inspiriting, Mr. Bemsher. Drifting across the water, I felt almost inflamed with enjoyment. The sight of all those floating flowers, gently bobbing up and down, fresh-plucked, fostered a strange fervor in me. The journey here aroused dark dreams and set astir odd inclinations."

"They're imported flowers," said Jolson.

"I'm Penny Enx," said the lovely girl. "Adopted daughter of Managing Warden Collis Enx."

"I recognized the style," said Jolson, starting to move away.

"I have a prison farm named after me."

"You deserve probably more." Jolson smiled and hurried on. He'd left the actual Linol Zee Bemsher in Warehouse 5; so 3 should be a couple of warehouses over.

"About those offensive pigs," called a brown lizard in a velvet-collared coat.

"Been taken care of," replied Jolson. He was passing a tent of jugglers when someone else yelled at him.

"Wait. Emergency," shouted a voice Jolson had been using himself until recently.

"Henry Carlos, we thought you were getting so forgetful as to miss my fête entirely," said Jolson, turning.

Henry Carlos Barby was in the same flowered dressing gown Jolson had left him in when he'd hidden him away in his mansion. "Political Espionage," said the cartoonist.

"Though I would have hoped you'd remember that white tie was, if not insisted on, strongly hinted at, Henry Carlos."

"Tied up by a PEO agent. Or a Chameleon Corps man."

"Indeed? That's very unsettling news."

"Any imposters?"

"There always are at a party this size."

"Impersonating me?"

"Why, no, Henry Carlos," said Jolson. He caught the political cartoonist's arm. "We'd better hurry right over to Warehouse 3 and check the safe. I've got the suitcase there."

"Good idea," said Barby. "Gave me two shots. Probably expected second was sleeping drug. Wasn't."

"Oh, so?" The damned Political Espionage Office medical staff had mislabeled.

"Both truth drugs. Double dose I got. I was tied up. Babbling truth. Cleaning woman heard. Got me out. Here I am."

"In the nick of time, Henry Carlos." They had reached Warehouse 3. "You're fleeter of foot than I. Rush in there and open the safe."

"At once." Barby dashed up the marble steps, dodged around two draped nymphs and ran through an arched doorway.

When Jolson got inside the high-vaulted room, Barby was pulling open the door of a safe set in the wall behind a cabinet loaded with salt and pepper shakers. "Is it still there, Henry Carlos?"

"Yes." He moved to close the door of the safe.

"Hold on. Let us double check." The suitcase, a big

pebbled black one with brass trim, was in the safe alone. Jolson reached around the political cartoonist and pulled the suitcase out. "You have certainly saved the day, Henry Carlos." He unsnapped the fastenings and looked into the suitcase. It was full of money. "Though I would appreciate it if you'd draw fewer pigs and stop sleeping with F.P."

Barby blinked. "What?"

Jolson hit him on the chin and Barby dropped. Jolson tied the political pundit with his robe sash and gagged him with his handkerchief. After hiding the big man behind a crate marked STUFFED GROUTS: ESMERALDA, BARNUM SYSTEM, CONTEMPORARY, Jolson trotted out into the night with the suitcase.

F. P. Smith, in white silk, was greeting arriving guests on the marble pier. "Linol Zee, dearest, where are you bound?"

"To the mainland for an emergency errand, F.P." He waved to the nearest boatman. "Here, I'm commandeering this launch for the moment. Take me over to my private railroad car at once."

F. P. Smith clasped her hands together between her breasts. "Why are you doing this in the middle of your birthday party?"

Jolson got himself and the suitcase of stolen money into the bright white launch. "Just a little whim," he said and sailed off across the flowers and dark water.